The Truth About Lies

For Dolf, James and Ally

STRIPES PUBLISHING
An imprint of the Little Tiger Group
1 Coda Studios, 189 Munster Road, London SW6 6AW

A paperback original
First published in Great Britain in 2018

ISBN: 978-1-84715-948-9

A CIP catalogue record for this book is available from the British Library.

Printed and bound in the UK.

10 9 8 7 6 5 4 3 2 1

The Truth About Lies

TRACY DARNTON

1

Dartmeet College, Devon, England

A liar ought to have a good memory.

English proverb

They make me go to counselling. It's been a month already but I still have to waste my afternoon with Dr Harrison at Mandela Lodge. The guy's an idiot. Maybe these sessions would be worthwhile if Dr Harrison was any good at his job, or if I was actually upset about Hanna dying, but he's not, and I'm not. But we pass the time both pretending to be otherwise.

"If only Hanna had told me how bad she was feeling," I say. "I could've helped." I dab my eyes with a tissue from the box placed carefully on the edge of my armchair. It's for the weeping mob hanging round his office. Girls like Maya and Keira who are enjoying the drama of it all. "I knew she was upset about breaking up with Ed, but I never thought…" I trail off, leaving a dramatic pause.

Dr Harrison reaches out and pats my hand. "None of us did. None of us saw the signs."

He's the one with the framed certificates in psychology and counselling on the wall so maybe *he* should have spotted something. After all, Hanna used to see him because of all her 'body issues'. Hanna – the most beautiful girl you've ever seen. But I let it go.

"I suppose you never really know what's going on inside someone else's head," I add, blowing my nose and seeing that the irony's completely lost on Dr Harrison as he nods sadly and passes me another tissue.

"You're not to blame yourself, Jess," he says. "You were a good friend and roommate to her."

I don't blame myself.

I blame Hanna.

You see, Hanna set this off. She started going out with Ed. Not because she'd found her soulmate, not because she couldn't live without him, but because she knew how much I liked him – and that I'd never dare to act on it. It was just another game for her. And because she was always able to click her fingers and have any student here panting after her, she took him. Just like that.

I saw them together in the lunch queue, leaning in towards each other, whispering, a touch on the arm, and I knew. It was exactly 12.55 p.m. on June 14th last term. A pleasant twenty-two degrees and sunny outside. We'd done maths that morning, pages 72 to 78 of the textbook, mine had a coffee stain on page 76. Hanna wore pink Converse pumps, a cute flowery dress and… I could go on and list every last detail in the dining hall and describe every single person who was there that Tuesday but it would take too long. You'd get bored. Jesus, I'd get bored.

So back to the late departed Hanna Carlsen. I pretended it didn't matter – the rubbing my nose in it. I forced a winning smile. I whispered to her later that they were so perfect together, made for each other. And she flicked her white-blond hair and fiddled with her friendship bracelets. But I stored it up. It can be hard for me to move on – to not bear a grudge.

I force myself to refocus on Dr Harrison. He's now suggesting a tablet if I'm having trouble sleeping. I take a special interest in pharmacology and physics these days. I test myself for fun to pass the time while Dr Harrison polishes his glasses and drones on about

3

post-traumatic stress disorder.

Question 1 (5 marks)

List the primary symptoms of a combination of alcohol, caffeine, appetite suppressants and low self-esteem.

Answer

Weight loss, blurred vision, tachycardia, nausea, confusion. (Open windows on the third floor to be avoided.)

Question 2 (5 marks)

How long would it take a teenage girl weighing seven stone to hit the ground when falling from a third-floor window?

Answer

No time at all. Even a skinny girl like Hanna makes a hell of a mess on impact.

*

I never thought the whole Hanna situation would end like that. She didn't have to get so obsessed with how she looked, so thin-skinned about any criticism. But one thing leads to another. One lie rolls on to more. Unintended consequences. And life is full of those.

Now Dr Harrison's fiddling with his bushy eyebrows and doing that annoying tongue-clicking again. He uses it to fill the silences in our sessions. But this time he's the first to crack and speak again: "It's tragic when young life full of promise is ripped away." He speaks like a packet of fortune cookies. "Bereavement casts a shadow that's slow to fade." And another one. "But time can heal." Boom. A hat trick of clichés. He should go into the greeting-card business or cheesy calendars. Maybe he is already and that's where he gets all these platitudes. They're meaningless.

Doesn't he realize he's meant to listen as a counsellor, not dish out his opinions? But I can't be bothered to explain this to him. I don't want to shake his world order. He looks attached to his dingy study in this college in the middle of nowhere and his life with his mousy wife. She smiles out shyly from the photo on his desk. He's moved it from the middle shelf since our last encounter.

"You can contact me at any time, Jess. Not just within these sessions." He takes a card from the drawer and pulls an old-fashioned fountain pen from his shirt pocket. His nib scratches in the awkward silence. "But let's meet again at five on Thursday. I've written it down so you don't forget."

"Thank you," I say, lip quivering as I carefully cup the card between my hands. "And thank you for listening."

I'm adorable. He loves this sort of rubbish. I swear his eyes are filling up as I close the door behind me.

I rip his stupid appointment card into tiny squares and let them flutter away on the breeze in the courtyard.

I don't need a piece of paper to remember anything.

2

Hyperthymesia – hyper (Anc. Gk: excessive) + thymesia (Anc. Gk: memory)

Every generation has its flashbulb moments. Events that are so major you always remember exactly where you were and what you were doing. Like when the planes hit the Twin Towers or a terrorist bomb ripped apart a Tube train. They're ingrained in your head. Flash-click. But can you remember where you were a week last Monday? A month ago? A year? Can you recall details about an ordinary day?

I can. For me, every waking moment is a flashbulb moment. I recall everything from the age of eleven like a never-ending motion picture. The interesting and the boring, the good and the bad. But especially the bad. I hold on to every cruel word, every act of unkindness, every act of betrayal. I have major baggage. Now imagine what that could do to a person. Your brain would explode, right? Or you might end up a bit like me.

Professor Coleman helped me to manage it, once upon a time, showed me how to file things away. She's a professor of cognitive neuroscience and I was her amazing guinea pig. So this is how I've learned to cope: I imagine the inside of my head is a vast library; a beautiful one with galleries and mezzanines and sliding ladders, flooded with daylight and with free vending machines. Everything I'd like an actual library to be. Why not? I have to carry it around with me *all* the time. The bookshelves are lined with all the books and journals I've ever read, courtesy of my photographic memory.

I can take down a virtual book, open it up and check what I read. All this I do in a millisecond. I'm a walking Wikipedia without the need for Wi-Fi.

But the biggest area in my mind-library is the 'Autobiography' section, thanks to my hyperthymesia. And this is where I'm truly unique. Here I have whole rooms labelled by year. Everything is filed, every single day has its own book – the date written neatly on the spine.

Say I want to know what I was wearing on January 18th 2015 (a Sunday, terrible weather). I go to the library in my head, make my way to the oak-panelled room for 2015, select the shelf for January, take down the book for January 18th and open it. All in my brain. And then I see it: a complete record of the day I can fast-forward or rewind: jeans, blue sweatshirt (nothing special).

I've made it sound controlled. It isn't. It can be hard to keep the memories filed tidily on the shelves. They fight for my attention, flooding me with a crazy rush of emotion. And if one gets loose, it brings more cascading down with it. All those minutes, hours, days of my life, jostling to be replayed.

On the way back from Mandela Lodge, I stop at the makeshift shrine in the courtyard to straighten a teddy bear. It's fallen over in the autumn breeze and is in danger of burning on the tea lights. We don't want another tragedy. The toy's rank but no one dares to throw any of this rubbish in the bin yet. Hanna was seventeen not seven.

'Heaven has a new angel' is on the latest bunch of flowers, still with a price sticker from the local garage shop. *So* classy. They've been doing a roaring trade in candles and cheap bouquets wrapped in plastic. People who didn't even know Hanna are wallowing in tribute Facebook pages and mock-religious rituals. The college is planning a sponsored hike across Dartmoor, working in teams 'like Hanna would have wanted'. Would she? Really?

The Principal must be wetting herself in fear that more worried parents will pull their kids out of the school. Five have gone already, including Ed. Not much fun being the ex-boyfriend of the girl who died. People stared and whispered. *I* stared and whispered. Accidental death or suicide, whichever one it was, isn't good for business for boarding schools. Dartmeet College is full of international kids and misfit British ones whose parents dump them here. Some choose the college because of its 'holistic, caring, international' mission statement. It claims to be educating the future leaders of aid organizations and global businesses and promoting world peace, blah, blah. I'm not sure how well that's panning out, but the old buildings certainly hook rich oligarchs looking for a Hogwarts experience for their little darlings. Although it turns out nobody appreciates *actual* death and drama.

I chose Dartmeet because it's remote and a long

way from my old life. And my mum liked the glossy brochure once upon a time.

I light the candles that have blown out and spot a new envelope addressed to Hanna. This one takes my attention for being edged in black ink like a Victorian mourning announcement. She won't be reading it herself so I may as well have it.

"Hi. Jess, isn't it?" The new guy Dan's standing there looking uncomfortable, his hands pushed deep into the pockets of his jeans. He looks even taller than his six foot two from my crouched position. "I wanted to tell you I'm really sorry about your friend," he says. He flicks his floppy gingery hair out of his eyes, and it falls right back again.

I shove the card quickly into my bag. He holds out a hand to help me up. He's strong but he doesn't look like a meathead – not like the rugby players. "You picked a bad time to join Dartmeet," I say.

He shrugs. "Circumstances. This is … nice." He points unconvincingly at the shrine.

"It's OK, you don't have to pretend. I know it's lame."

"If it helps, that's good," he says.

"Hanna would've liked it. She was into this sort of thing," I say. "She looked blond and pink but she could be quite dramatic. Gothic even." I smile. He smiles.

"Gothic?"

"She loved Halloween," I find myself saying, "and vampire movies." I'm just making stuff up.

He looks embarrassed, like he's run out of death small talk. "I was going to the Common Room to get a decent coffee. Want to come?"

He doesn't know yet that I'm not good company. I dislike all the chatter clogging up my head for evermore. The inconsequentiality of most conversations here is unbelievable. And if someone says something that irritates me, I'm stuck with it whirring around and around until I can subdue it in my mind-library, shove it on a shelf and lock the room.

So I was going to say no, be my usual self, but something about him makes me want to say yes for a change. And wouldn't that be the normal thing to do? I aim to come across as normal from time to time. Especially as I'm lacking in the pretend friends department after Hanna leaving me. Maya and Keira have taken me under their wing to demonstrate their compassion for the dead girl's roommate but it's not a comfortable place to be. My brain cells are slowly dying, for one thing. So I smile at Dan and say, "Sure," like a typical seventeen-year-old.

*

We take our coffees to a table out on the decking. In winter there are heat lamps and blankets but right now there's still just about enough warmth in the sun to sit outside. There's a good view of the well-kept gardens and the untamed moor beyond, with a distant silhouette of the tors that pass for hills in Devon.

Dan chats on about his room, makes me laugh about his roommate's rules on the storage of their footwear, tells me he had a nasty virus that kept him off school till now and how he's playing catch-up in his classes. He's easy to be around and I relax into the chair and sip slowly at my drink.

"Are you doing the vigil for Hanna tonight?" he asks.

"It might be too upsetting," I say. I fiddle with the ends of my hair, twirling my finger around and around. Why can't everyone move on? It's been four whole weeks already. Hanna's parents flew her body back to Denmark for a burial there. But the grief brigade felt cheated and so we had an interminable memorial service and now this 'vigil' in the chapel.

"These rituals are to help the living," he says. "My dad's a vicar so I've seen a lot of them. But if it makes matters worse for you, don't do it."

He makes it sound so easy.

13

"You're better than Dr Harrison," I say. "He's way out of his depth with all this."

"I can drone on for hours if nobody stops me but I'll shut up now. No one likes an armchair shrink." He smiles at me over his coffee cup and I notice the tiny freckles on his nose. "I want to study psychology at uni."

"That makes a change from the world-peace wannabes in this place who are all off to do sustainable development or geopolitical science," I say. "You can usually find them in the yoga yurt. Though I guess you'll be bringing peace, too – just one tortured soul at a time."

"Yes, it's a long-term plan," he says, grinning back. "I should be done by 2450." He checks his expensive-looking watch. "Gotta go in a minute. I said I'd go for a run with Felix."

I can't help but frown. I hope he's not a joiner-inner. Professor Coleman told *me* to get a hobby once upon a time. Something to distract me from the never-ending replay of my life to date. She gave me paints and pencils and one of those God-awful mindfulness colouring books. I was so beyond calming down with some pretty patterns – that was one of the ways she misjudged me.

One day, I guess I'll have it out with her. But it'll be on my terms. There's no rush. It's not like I'm going to forget.

3

Many would dispute the existence of true photographic or eidetic memory combined with hyperthymesia. But I studied extensively, all too briefly, a remarkable subject who exhibited complete recall of events since she was eleven years old, coupled with an eidetic memory. She was truly extraordinary.

Principles of Memory – *Professor A.E. Coleman*

On my way back to my room, I spy Maya and Keira but I'm too late to avoid them. As usual they manage to look as though they've stepped straight from the pages of a Hollister catalogue. Maya is basically a younger, hotter version of Rihanna – if Rihanna played netball and sprayed just the ends of her hair pink. And Keira specializes in perfectly straight brown hair and glisteningly white teeth. My new best friends: I can't stand either of them.

"Jess. There you are," says Maya, grabbing my arm. "I left training early. We've only got three hours to get everything ready."

I play dumb. "For?"

"For Hanna's vigil, silly. Keira and I thought we could all wear a red ribbon this time."

"To represent all the love that's coming out of this terrible thing," says Keira. "All the support we're giving each other." Keira and Maya hold hands and each stretch one out to me so I join their little circle of shiny, beautiful people. All I can think about is the three witches in *Macbeth* but I take their hands and count to twenty before letting go. That was enough time, I think. They seem pleased.

"I had an idea as well," I say, wondering if it's too ridiculous even for them. "I thought we could show how we're all working together…"

"Stronger together," says Maya solemnly.

"Absolutely… By physically building a wall," I say.

They look worried, maybe thinking I'm suggesting a spot of bricklaying to ruin their matching manicures.

"Out of Lego," I add. "Because she was Danish." I pause to let it sink in. "And all the different colours can represent all the different nationalities here at school."

I can see they're getting excited about it already. They were running low on ways to stretch out the whole grieving process.

"And we'd be making change one brick at a time, like the college mission statement," says Keira.

"It could be a Wall of Peace ... or a pagoda ... or a replica of the chapel," says Maya with a dreamy far-off look in her eyes.

"Or maybe a model of the Great Pyramid of Giza. With camels. That was Hanna's favourite holiday," I lie. I look sadly down at my shoes.

Maya hugs me and Keira goes to see if there's any Lego in the DT lab.

I make my escape from Tweedle Dumb and Dumber and go back to my room. My own room. I used to share a twin with Hanna so, as I said, unintended consequences. I literally just had to burst into tears in front of Principal Barker and it was job done. New room, no roommate. I picked a modern room in C-Block, well away from the third floor, with my own en-suite. It still has that fresh-paint, new-carpets smell, which I reduce with a rosemary diffuser and by leaving the window slightly open. The walls and blinds are plain white so I've added a pineapple-patterned duvet cover and a cushion for the desk chair. It's smaller than the twin rooms but I don't have as much stuff as most people my age so that's OK, and the view's not the best in college but you can't have everything.

I hum away to myself as I sort out clothes for the vigil. Nothing too showy, nothing too plain. I smear concealer on a couple of spots. I bet Maya's never had a blemish in her life. My hair looks smartest up so I loosely plait it and clip it at the back. I check myself in the mirror: every inch the devastated best friend. But I also look more like my mother, without the lipstick. Mum wore lip liner and red lipstick, even in her pyjamas over breakfast. She called it her warpaint, always ready to do battle with the world. She was what's technically called 'a pain in the arse' but she revelled in it. She taught me everything I know.

When Mum first took me, aged eleven, to our GP about my 'problem' she was typically itching for a fight. He was an impatient, grey-haired Scot with a large mole on his cheek, who enjoyed patronizing his patients. "Have I got this straight, Mrs Walsh? You've brought your daughter to see me because you think she's *too* clever?" he said.

I was sitting there, swinging my legs, silently memorizing all the titles on his bookshelf.

"She knows things she shouldn't be able to know yet," repeated my mother slowly. "A huge volume of facts."

"Children are sponges at this age," he said. "My own

son was obsessed with dinosaurs."

"But she remembers everything. Not just what she's read. What she's *seen*. She can remember a particular day – what was on the TV, what we were wearing, the weather. *Everything*. Tell him," she said, tugging at my arm. "Tell the doctor what you did a year ago today, for instance."

Too easy. It was a Wednesday. I was at school. It rained all morning. We read pages 45 to 60 of *Matilda* in class and talked about being nice to people. I ate a cheese sandwich and a banana for lunch. Boring. I didn't think the doctor would be interested in any of that so I kept quiet.

"Tell him!" Mum was working herself up.

"You've updated your edition of *Emergency Drugs in General Practice* since I came with tonsillitis fifty-eight days ago," I said. "And the cleaner still hasn't removed the dead ladybird in the corner of the window."

"See! It's weird, that's what it is," said Mum, and the doctor made a note. As usual with my mother and any interaction with authority, it ended with a row and her threatening to contact the *Daily Mail* over how he'd spoken to her. But it was also the beginning of the referral chain that led me to Professor Coleman and the Programme.

I shrug off the memories, carefully refile the metaphorical book and put it back on the shelf in my mind-library. I grab my lip balm from my bag. The black-edged envelope addressed to Hanna is still in there. I'm impressed by its sense of occasion – like it's been written by a fan of Tim Burton movies. I carefully rip it open with the edge of my thumb. Inside, written on black-edged card in sprawling cursive handwriting is one line:

I know you didn't jump

4

We do honestly repent and are sorry for our misdoings.
The remembrance of them is grievous unto us; the burden
is intolerable.

The Book of Common Prayer, *1662*

I have to admit, the chapel looks beautiful. The choir
stalls have the long candles lit and all around are
flickering pillar candles and wall sconces. The statue
of St Petroc is glowing, surrounded by tiny tea lights.
By the aisle, there's a framed photo of Hanna and a
vase of lilies on a table. I hate the sickly sweet smell of
lilies and Hanna was allergic to them, but never mind
because this whole charade has nothing to do with the
real Hanna. The mourners-in-chief Maya and Keira
are by the door like a reception line at a wedding,
holding it all together. They're handing out red ribbons

and forcing baskets of Lego on the congregation. A poor attempt at a multicoloured pyramid has its own table at the back. The 'Hanna Carlsen collaborative peace model'. Please!

"Hey, you came after all!" Dan's by my elbow as I add a few red bricks and a policeman mini-figure to the display.

"I'm here for Hanna," I whisper. Slightly true, but mainly I didn't want to stay in my room dwelling on the black-edged card.

The chaplain clears her throat and we quickly take a seat as she welcomes us all. She's Welsh with a gentle lilt and the perfect solemn voice for this occasion. Principal Barker, on the other hand, has a voice like fingernails on a blackboard and delivers a mercifully short reading of a Christina Rossetti poem. Her long grey hair is wound tightly into a bun and she's changed out of her usual hand-woven-by-deserving-orphans outfit to dress smartly in black.

After the choir sob their way through *Hallelujah*, and we recite a brief excerpt from the Book of Common Prayer, we come to the awkward 'vigil' when candles are handed out and we light our own from our neighbour's. Principal Barker talks about the Dartmeet community pulling together and supporting each other, one metaphorical brick at a time. We have some time for silent prayer or reflections when I think through my biology homework, but then we all have to sit there with our candles slowly dripping hot wax while Mr Humphries massacres Rachmaninov on the piano. This being a vigil rather than a service means we have to hang around for ages, holding candles, drinking hot chocolate provided by the kitchens. Occasionally a tearful member of staff or a student will share a special memory or read a poem and then we all go back to the waiting. Waiting for midnight so we can go. I guess it's as good a way as any for a bunch of sixteen-to-eighteen-year-olds stuck out on Dartmoor to pass a damp October evening.

My candle needs replacing and I get up to stretch my legs. I check out the Book of Condolence to see if anyone has thought of anything original to say. And then I spot it, in the middle of the penultimate page:

'And if thou wilt, remember

And if thou wilt, forget.'

Two lines from the Rossetti poem read by the Principal. But signed *HCC*. Hanna Camilla Carlsen. I scan faces to see who wrote in the book. Somebody in the chapel surely. I'm one messed-up bunny but even I don't think you should pretend to be Hanna at her own memorial vigil.

I take a new seat at the back, in sight of the Book of Condolence. As the clock strikes midnight, there's a spontaneous round of applause, like we accomplished something. A truly wonderful occasion which afterwards everyone hails as a great success and so very moving. There's an after-vigil party going down in B-Block with vodka and marshmallows but I pass. Maya and Keira decide to go but they completely understand if I'm 'too upset'. I'm a difficult person to be pity-friends with and they look as relieved as I am when I decline.

I kick around the cloisters for a bit, taking in the fresh air and the clear skies and the stars. When I first arrived here in January after what happened with Mum, I found it hard to adjust. It was so quiet after the noise of London. I missed the orange glow of the city and the rumble of traffic and intermittent sirens. But now I appreciate the quiet and darkness. I think it helps my unusual brain to keep on an even keel. Maybe that's what Mum saw in the place. The owls can be loud sometimes, shrieking like there's been a murder. And there are occasional night-time antics along the corridors between Lena, whose father is a Russian gas billionaire, and Makoto who's a gentle guy from Japan who hadn't met girls like Lena before. But mostly it's incredibly peaceful.

As soon as I get to my room, I know. I can picture in my head *exactly* how I left it earlier this evening. I know where the clothes were on the bed, the extent to which the drawers were left open and the arrangement of the items on the desk. Someone has been in here. Someone has opened drawers and cupboards, moved my papers, laid the jumper back on the bed instead of the chair. Nobody but me would know. It's basically Kim's game from that Kipling book. You've probably played an easier version at kids' parties. Items are put on a tray for you to memorize and then one is removed and you have to spot what's missing.

I'm good at Kim's game and all its variations. I mean *really* good at it. Professor Coleman trained me up. At the beginning, I enjoyed the tests and puzzles and *attention*. I guess it was flattering. I could be myself. I could show off. Everything I said and did was obsessed over, complimented. It was a whole new experience to have a group of people hanging on my every word and telling me how *extraordinary* I was.

Before Mum had pulled me out of school after a series of stand-up rows with the Head, I'd spent a lot of time sitting by myself working my way through the school library. I didn't really have friends there. I couldn't forget when they were mean to me or excluded me or didn't pick me for the rounders team. I couldn't understand how they all managed to get along, how friendships were broken one minute and fixed the next, how they moved on so easily.

But as the visits to the Programme increased, soon I was a freak show or circus act. I was a clever puppy made to jump through ever-increasing hoops. Take Kim's game: first we did it with objects like the party game but increasing by fifty each time, then we did it with data – reams of data, names and addresses where one detail would be changed slightly, then satellite topographical pictures, and on and on. My latest trick was never enough – they always wanted me to do more.

And overseeing it all, like a queen bee, was Professor Coleman.

5

*Does everyone have an untapped store of vivid images
and memories? Do we all have the capacity for the perfect
memory, if only we had the key to retrieval?*

Principles of Memory – *Professor A.E. Coleman*

I wake and lie staring at the ceiling as the daylight
slowly creeps around the blinds. I wonder who's been
poking around my room and leaving black-edged
notes and tasteless messages in condolence books for
their entertainment.

I read once how the Stasi in East Germany used
to break into people's apartments and move things
around, or take worthless items away. They were
messing with the heads of potential enemies of the
state, to make them doubt their own state of mind.
Simple but effective, though requiring a supremely

callous disregard for your own citizens. But that technique would never have worked on me. I have the certainty that my recollection is one hundred per cent correct. When I was first diagnosed by Professor Coleman, she made it sound like it was a superpower but I was disappointed that it wasn't as cool as flying or X-ray vision. It took me a while to see it had potential.

Mum, on the other hand, was sure it wasn't a good thing from the start. "Finally someone gets it," she said to Coleman, pursing her perfect lips, outlined with her usual red lipstick. "Now what are you going to do about it?"

"Observe her. Conduct research," said Coleman. "There have been so few people across history with your daughter's level of memory, Mrs Walsh. The photographic nature of her memory is exceptional enough but my interest lies in the autobiographical memory – the hyperthymesia." She sounded out the six syllables. Coleman had a way of rubbing Mum up the wrong way by talking to her like she was a complete fool.

"I meant, what are you going to do about making her better?" said Mum, fixing the professor with her hard stare reserved for obstructive council officials.

Coleman had laughed. "This is a supreme talent, Mrs Walsh, not an illness."

But looking back, I've often thought Mum had it right.

*

I skip breakfast but I'm still late for my lesson – Theory of Knowledge, TOK for short. I sneak in at the back of the classroom with the other latecomers. The post-vigil party must have been a success as there are some bleary-eyed students here. Ms Macfarlan's TOK class is usually the ideal opportunity for a gentle snooze. But there's a different feel about the class today and it doesn't need my brain to notice that Ms Mac has been replaced by a new, younger teacher. He's wearing a tweed jacket and cords as though he's come straight from a shooting party on the moor, or the Oxford debating society. He says he's standing in for Ms Macfarlan and writes 'Ramesh Desai' on the board. He makes us all introduce ourselves like we're at junior school and then says, "Good morning," and repeats our names back.

"Theory of Knowledge: how do we know what we know?" he says. "I understand you've been looking at perception and language so far. We'll be exploring objective and subjective knowledge and what we choose to hang on to." He's clearly able to rely on his good looks for popularity as he breaks the rule for new teachers and hands out a test paper straight away. "But our first focus is memory as a way of knowing. Names on papers please, but I shan't be giving grades for this – it's purely for discussion."

A few people titter as they work their way through the questions. They range from giving your best friend's phone number to the capital of Bolivia. I write down Hanna's number before thinking about it. I wonder if I'd get her 'please leave a message' voice or if her parents have cancelled the phone contract and wiped out the last echo left of her. Obviously I could get full marks on Mr Desai's general knowledge questions but I choose not to. I've learned it's never a good idea to be exceptional, to be extraordinary.

It always amazes me how little ordinary people know. Even with deliberately flunking some questions, I do better than nearly everyone.

Mr Desai sits on the edge of his desk and thumbs through the test papers. "These are not impressive. Your brains are doing so many different things at once but the secret to good retention and retrieval is concentration. You need to let your brain focus on the facts you want it to absorb. Otherwise it will discard information immediately and that info has no chance of making it into your long-term memory."

He points at each of us in turn and repeats our names. "An easy trick. I merely paid attention when you told me your names, repeating them to myself, adding a visual image. So Felix I imagine holding his cartoon cat namesake, Dan in a karate suit as *dan* is a ranking system in martial arts, and so on."

Impressive for a normal person. Maya's staring at him with her mouth open like he's a wizard.

"If you make your brain work at it, your retention will be better, in all your subjects," says Mr Desai. "Your homework, folks: a thousand words on 'We are delegating our memory. Discuss.'"

Maya's already got her hand up to say she doesn't understand.

Mr Desai takes a breath. "Your generation is content to delegate retention of facts to your phone, Wikipedia, Siri, Cortana, Alexa, *anyone.*" He holds up one of the papers. "And most of you can't even remember an eleven-digit phone number. You merely tap the name of the person you're calling on your handset. It's no wonder you don't know the dates for the Civil War or South American capitals. Most people find it difficult to retain more than seven items in short-term memory. Some research suggests the figure is closer to four."

He pauses and looks around at us. He's way more intense than Ms Mac, who preferred to talk about patriarchal views of knowledge and women lost to history.

"You, my little tech-freaks, have deskilled, contracted out, *given up* your own memory, your autonomy. And you're too busy checking your Facebook page to even care about it. Discuss."

He has *my* attention at least. I've never understood the love my contemporaries have for their technology but then I'm not reliant on it in the same way. I actually prefer the written page, flicking through real books in the college library, to browsing online; I'm old-fashioned like that. I can absorb a whole shelf in an evening if the mood takes me. Flash-click. Whereas all those Internet links online can be overwhelming for my type of brain, straining to take on every fact it sees, going down endless alleys of information. I have to pace myself.

Mr Desai picks up Keira's phone and waves it at us like it's infected. "At the current rate of technological progress, and as our brains adapt, what will happen to our memory systems? Or am I wrong and you actually know your top-dialled numbers? What about a poem? Anything beyond the first two lines?"

He's speaking with an unnerving intensity now, leaning forward, his brown eyes sparkling. "Is it happening?" asks Mr Desai, slamming the phone back on the desk. "You bet it is! Does it matter? That's what I want to see your thoughts on."

The bell goes for the end of the lesson, chairs shoot backwards. Mr Desai raises his voice over the din. "One thousand words by next session. And don't forget." He places the test papers in his briefcase. Maya laughs coquettishly at his terrible joke.

*

The chat all day is about Ramesh Desai. Where's he from, is that an East Coast American accent, is he married, how old is he? Is he living on-site? Is it legal to perv over a supply teacher and vice versa? How does he keep his skin so smooth? Does he work out, to be so buff? The consensus is everyone hopes Ms Mac has a long absence.

I've soon had enough of the noise and mindless gossip. After supper, I retrieve my bag from the pile at the entrance to the dining hall and retreat to the college library. I always pick the small table with two chairs (one for me, one for my bag to discourage company) tucked out of sight by the 'W to Z' in the fiction section. I can see the courtyard below, the comings and goings at Mandela Lodge and the librarian on a fag break. Here I can read my way through the books, transferring them from the Dartmeet musty shelves to my own mind-library of loveliness, one volume at a time. It limits me dwelling on the past.

I start with my biology homework and dig out the textbook. A postcard flutters out on to the table in front of me: a picture of Haytor Rocks on Dartmoor. The reverse has a single handwritten sentence:

THINGS ARE SELDOM WHAT THEY SEEM

"Found you!" It's Maya. "You look pale, Jess. Are you feeling all right?" She moves my bag off the chair and sits down without asking. "Headache?"

"Yes. Migraine coming on," I say, slipping the card back into the book.

"Bummer. Maybe you should have a scalp massage. I can do it. Felix said I'm really good at massage." She whispers, "Though I wasn't just massaging his head."

"No thanks. I'm best off sitting here quietly."

"Have you seen how big the Lego model is getting? It was *such* a good idea of yours." She fishes out her phone. "I've been looking at pictures of models online. It's so therapeutic for everybody, building something together. The camels are going to be tricky. It's weird but there are no curved bricks, just…"

"Bricky bricks?"

"Yes. You obviously know way more about it than I do." She smiles at me with her trusting puppy face. I know way more about *everything* than she does, except piano grades and how to play Goal Attack in netball. She's returned to her phone, scrolling through pages while talking. "Are you doing that essay yet for Mr Desirable? That's what Keira and I thought we should call him. We've been starved of a teacher under thirty for too long."

"Yes. I was about to get started on it. You know, really concentrate in the quiet." Hint effing hint.

"Why jam your brain with stuff you can look up really easily?" says Maya. "That's what I think. I just need to stretch out my theory for the thousand words somehow."

I'm worried that she's settling down to stay here. In my corner.

"We could do it together. Neither of us should be alone at A Time Like This." She tilts her silly head to one side and holds a sad-face pose. Then she waves wildly. "Over here, Keira!"

Keira's towing Dan, her arm linked through his. Poor bloke.

"I'm making sure Dan knows his way around the library," Keira says, pointing at the shelves. "This is where all the books are kept, Dan."

Of course, the fact that Dan is an athletic, exceptionally good-looking, nice guy has *nothing* to do with Keira's wish to help with orientation. I don't remember her taking such an interest when that spotty kid Sean with the squint arrived from Arizona.

I sense Dan's trying to wriggle free of Keira's wrestling hold. He grins at me. For a moment, he has a look of the lovely Ed about him. "And this must be the happening area of the Dewey system," he says.

"Definitely. How about a library par-ty!" says Maya. "I'll message everyone."

"It's a school night," I find myself saying, like I'm a fifty-year-old woman in a cardigan. "And it's the library." I put my finger on my lips.

"Libraries – where shhh happens," says Dan, which makes Keira laugh as though it's the funniest thing she's ever heard.

A loud 'shush' travels over the stacks from the direction of the librarian's desk. She's back from her nicotine fix.

"Shhh," adds Maya, then Dan, then all around the

library is a riot of shhh-ing and giggling. They are so rock and roll.

And then I think I should play the Hanna-grief card to get rid of them. I guess at some point I won't be able to. What's the timescale for getting over a death? One month? Two months? A year? There must be a graph drawn up somewhere with closeness of relationship on one axis and time passed on the other. For normal people, time heals as memories fade. But what if, like me, your memories are so sharp that you can still see a person in your head like they're in front of you? Still smell them like they're in the room? What if they follow you everywhere?

"Shut up! Shut the hell up!" someone is shouting at the top of their voice. It turns out to be me.

6

Many of us have an ability to 'see' an image for a short while after it's taken away. For a rare few, this 'eidetic imagery' or photographic memory persists for many years.
Principles of Memory – *Professor A.E. Coleman*

I'm here again. Mandela Lodge. The flowery armchair with the tissues. This time the Principal is along for the ride, which has sent Dr Harrison into a cheesy show of caring concern. Today he gives me a cup of tea *and* a biscuit.

We all sit balancing a mug and a custard cream and listening to the clock tick until Principal Barker gets the ball rolling. "Jess, we've shown you a certain amount of understanding, given both the tragic death of Hanna and your own difficult home circumstances."

By which she means I don't actually have a home,

except here. Not that she knows the half of it.

"But obviously the librarian cannot turn a blind eye to that sort of behaviour and language," she adds.

Language? I barely said anything. Anyway, libraries are just the place for language. Why, there are 228 instances of 'bad language' in *Catcher in the Rye* alone. And that's on the library shelf. But it's not the right time for this discussion. They may be disturbed to know I count swear words in modern classics when I can't sleep.

"But obviously we're concerned about whether you're coping after losing your friend. And I still haven't been able to speak directly to your guardian yet," continues Barker.

"He travels all the time," I say. "He's hard to get hold of." Especially as I made him up.

"I have sent him emails," she says.

To which I always reply within a decent interval. I'll be eighteen in January, after which my fictitious guardian can retire. Then I'll take the International Baccalaureate Diploma in the summer and head off into the wide blue yonder. Maybe college in the States. I'll put the Programme and my past behind me.

"Dr Harrison and I are wondering if a sabbatical would be appropriate? To give you some time to get over what happened to Hanna," says Barker. Is her concern really for me or for the college? They want normality restored. They don't want screaming in the library. Neither do I. Maybe I'm more freaked out by recent events than I thought.

"I wonder if there are other issues at play. From your life before you joined us at Dartmeet…" Dr Harrison checks my file. "In January. So, just over nine months ago." He's enjoying his moment in the limelight, showing off all the psychobabble he's picked up over the years. "Sometimes a recent tragedy – like Hanna's death – can stir up things that happened to us in the past which we've tried to forget."

He has no idea. He isn't up to the task of unravelling what's happened with me.

"Sometimes a divorce…?" he suggests.

I nod sadly for his benefit. He thinks he's hit the crux of the matter. He glances at Principal Barker, looking for approval. Mum got divorced when I was six months old. He wasn't even my dad in the first place. That's why they got divorced. I can't miss something I never had.

"Post-traumatic stress disorder is not to be taken lightly," says Dr Harrison. "You don't have to make a decision today but think about the time-out option.

You're young. A few months out at your age won't matter in the long term."

But he's wrong. It does matter. I'm staying put. I don't have anywhere else to go.

"Or maybe extra counselling sessions with you instead," I say. Dr Harrison's eyes light up and he grows taller in his chair, glancing again at Barker with a smug smile on his lips. He's bound to drop the dumb sabbatical idea now. "It's really helping," I say as earnestly as I can.

Barker looks at both of us. I wonder if she, like me, is not convinced that more time with Dr Harrison would be of any help to anyone. But I've handed her an easy solution, which means she can get back to her yoga mat and tofu. "That's settled then," she says, draining her cup and standing up to go. Another problem crossed off her 'To Do' list. Her duty done.

All this psychobabble means I have to run to make the start of the TOK lesson. Mr Desai's standing at the door to the classroom with a tray. "All phones please, all electronic devices, headphones. We're going to rely on our natural resources today."

There are grumbles but the class play along. Maya makes an elaborate gesture of saving me the seat next to her, hugging me and whispering loudly, "Are you

OK now?" So embarrassing. This sort of situation triggers memories of *other* times I've been embarrassed, too. They are so immediate, so *real*, that soon I'm a blushing, shaking mess of embarrassment until I get a grip and shove the recollections of those days back on the shelves of my mind-library. Each new time this happens the feelings are compounded – I now have the feeling of the remembering from today to add to the initial memory. A small snowball rolling and rolling gathering more snow until it's an enormous scary avalanche of emotion. I force the last memory on to the shelf and refocus.

Mr Desai's collecting in our essays. Makoto's talking to him in a low voice and showing him something. His English isn't fluent yet, and he's pretty shy, but Mr Desai leads him to the front and asks him to talk to the class about what inspired his essay. The final assessment includes an oral presentation so he wants us to practise.

Makoto shows us photo albums made from stiff card with tissue paper and tassels. He passes them around the class while he talks. "When I came here, I hadn't lived anywhere but Japan. I hadn't been away from my family."

Maya turns the pages for us when one reaches our

table, revealing black-and-white photos of people in Japan, some traditionally dressed, some men in uniform, other more candid shots of babies. I look at the family groups, long-dead, huddled in their best clothes, staring down the camera lens. Ghosts and spectres.

"I enjoy looking at these, seeing my family, my ancestors," says Makoto.

The next album is from the sixties or seventies. Fading colour shots and Polaroids of flares and miniskirts, kids on beaches with doting parents. I've never really bothered with photos since this memory of mine kicked in – I don't need them – and since leaving the Programme I'm careful not to appear on any, not to leave a trace of myself.

"Now in my family we take selfies," says Makoto. "We share them briefly but we never print them or make albums."

Mr Desai's encouraging Makoto to expand his idea, talking about the way images are stored and our reliance on technology which is soon replaced.

"I'm overwhelmed by the number of images," says Makoto. "I can't sort through those thousands of images. I can't tackle the, what's the word?"

"Backlog?" suggests Mr Desai.

"Yes, backlog."

At least it's possible to edit photos. I wish I could edit out my memories, rather than have this mountain of images.

"But the longer you leave it…" says Maya.

"You need discernment in what you choose to keep," says Mr Desai. "You guys aren't curating your life for the next generation in the same way that Makoto's relatives have here." He holds up an open album.

"It's so much effort," says Felix. "They've invested in this and made it something important. Camera, film, processing, choosing the album, choosing the best photos or the ones with meaning."

"And that's harder to do with a huge volume of material," says Makoto.

"And you have the same difficulty with knowledge," says Mr Desai. "When there is so much information at your fingertips, how do you sort out the important from the trivial, the truth from the lies, from the alternative facts?"

Makoto collects the albums together and holds them to his chest. "My great-aunt's nurse, she found these in an old suitcase that was being thrown out. Finding the albums in the trash was … er, *sachi*," he says. The guy's struggling with his English again. Blank faces in the class.

I consult my Japanese dictionary in my mind-library. "Serendipity," I say. "*Sachi* means serendipity." I absorbed words from Japanese and Russian on the Programme. The role of a super-memory in language-learning was one of the early research topics that excited Professor Coleman.

"Serendipity," repeats Makoto, tripping over the consonants slightly. "So I bring them with me to England because it reminds me that there are many before me, even though I had to pay excess baggage." He does a small bow and we all clap.

"I didn't know you speak Japanese, Jess," says Maya.

I realize I've broken my rule about never being exceptional. "I can't. I know some vocab from a friend I used to have, that's all."

"A pretty brainy friend," says Maya. "What does serendipity even mean in English?"

"Most people can just say hello, goodbye, thank you and two beers please," says Dan.

"Look around you," I say. "Dartmeet's international." But I know I've shown too much. I'm slipping.

7

*Did you ever play the 'I went to market and I bought...'
listing game as a child? Or 'Aunt Sal went on holiday
and she packed...'? How about 'Jess packed ... a one-eyed
teddy, a pendant and a wooden box'?*

Work Your Memory

The Dartmeet swimming pool looks almost pretty in
the evening. The underwater lights are on, picking out
the mosaic tiles at the bottom of the pool. The glow
reflects on the wall of windows that look out on to the
darkness of the gardens and the night sky. I sneak here
after hours and defy the 'Never swim alone' health and
safety sign. I swim up and down, counting lengths. It's
hypnotic. I like the rush of the water in my ears and the
weightlessness. The déjà vu of completing lengths is a
mindless repetition for me as I reach for the wall and
spin-turn, kicking my legs in a fizz of bubbles again

and again. It's the way I 'relax'. I guess it's my form of meditation or mindfulness, which Barker and Dr Harrison are always forcing on us. For me, the appeal is mind*less*ness. I focus on the breaths and the strokes and calm my brain.

One of Professor Coleman's assistants, Nadia, got me hooked on swimming, teaching me front crawl and how to breathe on every third stroke. We swam together every morning before she tested me on the type and volume of things I could remember.

But Nadia wasn't there for long. She was far too nice. Plus dissent and strong opinions were not tolerated by Coleman and I overheard them arguing. They went silent when I entered the room, and Nadia was red-eyed. She wasn't at the next session. Then the new assistant Brett arrived and the focus of the research shifted to *how* memories were laid down and reconsolidated. He had very different methods from Nadia. I swear he got a kick out of all the uncomfortable stuff he put me through.

One day I was pleased when he said we'd be playing games but it turned out to be visuospatial task games to be played *after* he'd inflicted various bad experiences on me. I'd play Tetris in the lab wearing my usual blue rubber cap with sensors while he tested me.

The emphasis was on post-traumatic stress disorder memories. I guess Brett was there to provide the trauma. That was my new routine.

I shake the memories away again. I've tried so hard to shut those times away but they keep pressing in, forcing me to relive them.

Now I break the lengths and float on my back in the darkness, my head cushioned by the water, ears half-submerged. I need the break from the stimulation of my senses.

"Is it a private pool or can anyone dive in?"

I start and lose my buoyancy in an ungraceful splash. I scramble to stand up, but the pool's too deep here. As I resurface, spluttering, Dan's standing by the shallow end.

"Sorry, I didn't mean to startle you." He holds up a hand in apology.

I swim to the ladder and climb out, shivering, reaching for my towel. "It's one a.m. You scared me half to death," I say. "No one's meant to be in here."

"*You* are. I saw the door was ajar. Do they always leave the fire exit open?"

"Yes, but not the changing rooms so..." I slip my hooded surfer towel over my head and start changing in front of him. I expect him to turn away embarrassed while I wriggle out of my costume under the towel. But he holds my gaze. I'm wishing I'd paid better attention to shaving my legs, even though it's pretty dark. "I couldn't sleep," I say. "I come here rather than lying in bed, staring at the ceiling."

"Guilty conscience?" He hands over my neat pile of clothes from the bench. "Or too much cheese before bed?" I stand there in my enormous towel, hugging the clothes to me. "I'll, er, give you some privacy," he says, turning away to face the windows.

"I've got in the habit of not sleeping since…"

"Since Hanna?" Dan turns back as I slip my jumper on. I realize he's been watching my dim reflection in the glass.

I say nothing and let him think that. I haven't slept well for ages. The Programme messed with my sleep patterns by exploring whether sleep deprivation would affect my ability to remember.

"Is this where all the insomniacs hang out, or just you?" he asks.

"Just me. And now you." I rub my hair with the towel while the secret hangs between us. "I'd rather you didn't say anything. Barker's on my case already."

I don't like asking for favours. They end up having

to be repaid.

"Sure. I won't tell if you won't." He reaches over and wipes a drip from my cheek.

I tremble or shiver; I'm not sure which. "And what exactly are *you* doing here at one o'clock in the morning?"

"I realized I'd left my watch in the gym."

Of all the crappy reasons to be sneaking around at night. "That woke you up, did it?"

"It was a gift," he says. "From someone special. I wanted to get it back."

From someone special. I step back and gather my stuff together. My necklace falls from the pile and lands right at his feet. He picks it up and dangles it from his hand, the pendant spinning softly. "That's unusual. I admired it when I saw you wearing it yesterday. Is it a pearl?"

"A black South Sea pearl. The chlorine in the pool would damage it so I take it off to swim." I hold out my hand but he's still examining it in the half-light. I don't want anyone else handling it. It belonged to my mother.

"May I?" He lifts my hair and fastens it around my neck. I can feel goose pimples spreading down my arms as he says quietly, "So how can I apologize for nearly drowning you? How about a trip out at the weekend? You can show me the bustling metropolis of Ashburton."

If he hadn't just told me about the 'someone special' I'd think he was asking me out. But he must mean as friends. Christ, I'm turning into Keira, losing my senses over a good-looking guy turning on the charm. I think it's better for all concerned if I don't get close to someone. And yet Dan…

"It's late, so…" I point at the door. "Make sure you pull it shut when you go." Before he can answer I slip out and run across the damp grass back to the accommodation blocks.

*

Back in my room, I realize the encounter with Dan has made me even less inclined to sleep. I sit up in my pyjamas and switch the light back on. I retrieve the two cards from their hiding place and look at them carefully again. The mourning card *I know you didn't jump* addressed to Hanna and the postcard THINGS ARE SELDOM WHAT THEY SEEM slipped into my bag.

Puzzling, but should I be worried by them? Are they connected, or is it a silly prank by someone gearing up for Halloween? The shrine and the vigil have encouraged people to be melodramatic and morbid. That's all it is.

Though it's funny how they've started just when Dan arrived.

8

Try the following memory exercise: Read each word once. Close the book and write down as many as you can remember:

friendship	*drink*
open	*window*
scream	*blood*
guts	*guilt*

Work Your Memory

I hate the great outdoors. Maybe because I grew up with a dog-turd-covered triangle of grass opposite our house to explore, but probably because I prefer the certainty of streets and buildings. I'd be a brilliant London taxi driver (aside from my lack of interpersonal skills and driving licence) because I actually have 'The Knowledge' of London streets and routes. Black-cab drivers take three years to learn it, zooming around on a moped with a clipboard. I don't want to brag, but I covered their Blue Book in a few days.

I know the Ordnance Survey maps for the area

around Dartmeet. The roads and towns are easy enough, but the moor itself is tricky. Too much empty space with no distinguishing features. The landscape changes according to the season, and one wet bog looks pretty much the same as all the others. Large areas of the map are plain green with contour lines and nothing more than 'cairns' or 'stones (remains of)' marked. How are you meant to have a clear picture in your head?

But there's no avoiding Dartmoor with Hanna's Hike. Keira and Maya are in overdrive organizing it with Dr Harrison, who was probably in the Scouts. He thought it would 'do me good' to be one of the organizers and to enter a team. It is not 'doing me good'. So far, even this meeting is annoying. Why did it have to be outside, staring at the moor and shivering in the drizzle? He's working out a route, pointing at the distant tor, a mass of granite at the highest point we can see from the college grounds. "Shall we include the old mine-workings before sweeping round past the reservoir?" he asks. "It's good to have points of interest."

Points of interest? It's a wilderness.

"Then we can carry on along the river and over Ryders Bridge?" he adds.

I'm only here to show willing and convince Harrison and Barker that I'm fine. I didn't know I'd actually have to contribute. Luckily Maya's here, and she can't be quiet for more than two minutes, so she can answer his route-planning suggestions while I nod wisely. Shouts travel from the rugby match on the playing fields. There are plenty of kids who've come here from minor public schools and think a weekend isn't a weekend without the chance to grind your classmate's face into the mud. I switched from team sports to the shooting club last term. There's something strangely satisfying about firing at little discs pretending to be pheasants. The Saturday running club has already streamed past in a blaze of Lycra. Running isn't for me either. I soon pulled out of that – I'm not keen on things I'm bad at. I'll stick to swimming. By myself. I have perfectionist traits. I brood forever on my failures, reliving coming last in a race over and over. Teachers feed you a lie that it's not about the winning or the losing, it's the taking part. That's so not true. I only play at anything if I have a fighting chance of winning.

I yawn after my lack of sleep last night. Keira's airhead grasp of organization isn't firing me up to stay alert. Her latest idea is to link up with the marines from the Commando Training Centre at Lympstone.

"They're always doing exercises on the moor and they help with the Ten Tors competition," says Keira. "And they're hot," she mouths while Dr Harrison disappears behind a map he's having trouble refolding.

"But this is *our* challenge for people who actually knew Hanna," says Maya.

"I agree with Maya. This is a Dartmeet College event. A low-key event," says Dr Harrison. "Not an endurance race."

"It's Hanna's Hike," says Maya, who would have gone for anything we'd come up with as long as it had alliteration and a T-shirt opportunity. Hanna's Hula-Hooping, Hanna's Hopscotch, Hanna's Hair-Straightening. Hanna's face smashed into the cobbles flashes into my memory again. I can see the mess. I can smell the mess.

"Jess? Jess?" Maya's waving her hands in my face. "Tune in, what do you think? Bring in the marines or not?"

"Not," I say, trying to look like I'm bothered either way.

"That's decided, then. We need marshals, water points…"

I tune out again. I don't want all this trivia swimming around my head forever. Turns out Hanna's more trouble dead than alive.

I really don't care what colour the T-shirts will be, but to stop Maya and Keira going through all the options I lie and say that Hanna's favourite colour was lime-green. Maya looks terrible in citrus colours and I can tell she's wavering so I add a few lip quivers to seal the deal.

They fix the date for Saturday November 5th. Mainly so that there can be fireworks and sparklers afterwards like we're a bunch of ten-year-olds.

"We can have a huge bonfire in the paddock and get the kitchens to do hot dogs and toffee apples. Perfect," says Keira.

"Do you think Hanna would like that?" Maya asks me, with that intense face she does so well, her brown eyes fixing on mine.

Hanna's dead. She doesn't think, she doesn't express opinions, she doesn't have to run round the moor freezing her bits off to earn a jacket potato and a look at a Catherine wheel. But I don't say this. I play nice. "She'd have loved it," I say in my most sensitive tone of voice. That is partially true. Certainly not the hike on Dartmoor, but she'd have liked being wrapped up in her Danish jumpers and hats and the whole 'hygge' vibe of fire and candles and hot drinks outside in the crisp air.

Most of all, she'd have liked being the centre of attention.

Hanna always did.

9

Remembering events is different to remembering facts.
You get just one shot to ingrain an event.

Principles of Memory – *Professor A.E. Coleman*

I need to get supplies from town. I say 'town', but Ashburton is basically two bisecting streets with limited shopping opportunities. If you need a waxed jacket, a cream tea and a Dartmoor tea towel, it is *the* place to go. Not so great for a seventeen-year-old. But needs must. I can't hide in Dartmeet College all the time or I'd die of boredom.

After the swimming-pool episode I've been avoiding Dan but he's standing outside the dining room rattling car keys. "Jess, Ashburton awaits," he says, as though I *agreed* to go with him.

Keira can't hide her surprise and her usually perfect pout settles into a thin line. Excellent. Why shouldn't he be interested in hanging out with me? It's obvious that Keira's put out and regrets committing to make Hanna's Hike posters all afternoon with Maya. So although I hadn't planned on going anywhere with Dan, it suddenly has the added bonus of annoying Keira *and* freeing me from an afternoon dodging the dimwits.

"You didn't mention you had a car," I say, pleased that we won't be having to take the rickety bus that takes three times as long. Maybe Dan isn't so bad. A rich kid who can drive could definitely come in handy. But when we reach the car park and I see the actual vehicle, I'm not so excited. It's a rust-bucket ancient Mini.

I think Dan can sense my disappointment by the way I'm staring at the car and making no effort to open the door and get in it. "Did you think I'd have a Porsche or a Ferrari?" he says.

"Is it even safe? I mean, should we take the bus anyway? Do you even *fit* in there?"

Dan lays a hand on the roof of the car. "Now we're hurt, aren't we, Uja?"

"Uja?"

He points at the registration: UJA 658K.

He unlocks the door by physically turning the key – no electronic beeping here. But the passenger door needs pushing open from the inside. "Take a seat, while I warm her up."

He turns the ignition and fiddles with the choke. "Sometimes I have to flip the bonnet and wallop the solenoid with a hammer," he says proudly. The engine whirrs into action. "But not today. She must like you." He gently revs the accelerator. "Look at the windows – wind-up handles. The back ones you push out on a hinge. Vintage."

"And this is a good feature?" I say.

"Wait till you see how she drives. You'll love her too. Have you passed your test?"

I don't want to push my luck and apply for a licence. It might attract the wrong sort of attention – from Coleman. "Not yet," I say. "Busy, busy."

Dan eases out of the parking space and on to the long, tree-lined drive down to the road. His enormous frame fills the car, his seat pushed back as far as it'll go. "I fixed her up myself. She was a real heap when I got her. My dad bought me Meccano and electronics kits when I was a kid. This is a big version of that."

His whole face has become animated, excited. About

a car. I would never have guessed he was a petrolhead.

"I like seeing how things work. Underneath. You don't get that with sealed-unit modern cars." He pats the dashboard affectionately.

"But you want to be a psychologist," I say. "Not an engineer or a mechanic?"

"Stripping down an engine and putting it back together so it works better – pretty much the same thing as psychotherapy." The clutch groans as he grapples with the gearstick. "It's all seeing what goes on underneath the surface."

I exhale as always on leaving the Dartmeet College bubble for a few hours. It's one of those rare sunny days with blue skies and changing colours in the gorse and the sprinkles of woodland. We pause for a couple of Dartmoor ponies as they meander across the road, unhurried by the gentle beep of the horn.

We motor on, thundering over the occasional cattle grid until Dan slows for a 'Blocked Road' sign as a traffic policeman flags us down.

"Stupid pony again," says the police officer. "Took out a farm vehicle which spilled silage all over everywhere. Take the high moor road instead."

We pull over so Dan can rummage under my seat for a dog-eared road atlas. "I'm not sure Uja would survive a collision with a furry pony," he says. "No satnav and there's no phone signal. We'll have to try the old-fashioned, vintage method: map-reading."

The road map's pages are crinkled and stained with coffee. I don't need it anyway. I chuck it on the back seat.

"It's that way," I say, pointing at the small turning off behind us.

"So did the bus often take this route? I can't imagine it did," says Dan as we bump along the track. "And I know you don't go running. Do you have an amazing sense of direction?"

"I've looked at the map before."

"What? And that's enough?"

I nod.

"So have you got a photographic memory? There was a boy at my junior school with that. Is that why you knew the Japanese word the other day?"

I hesitate. I've never denied having a photographic memory if someone asks outright, but not come clean on how good it is. It's the least exceptional part of my memory, after all. The autobiographical side, that's the really bizarre bit. "I don't like to show off about it," I say. "Turn right here."

"Why don't you ever talk about it?" he says. "If I had

a photographic memory, I mean, wow."

"What? You'd never shut up? Oh, wait, you never shut up anyway."

"Funny!" He flicks my arm with his fingers. "Can you really remember that map? All of it? Do you see it in your head?"

"Sort of. The roads are easy. The moor's more difficult – not enough features."

"Can you count cards? Could you win us loads of money in a casino?"

"No," I lie. "If this is turning into an extended road trip we need some music." I'm regretting telling him about my memory now. I fumble with the car radio and hissing static of Radio Devon until I work out the cassette player. The Beatles blast through the tinny speakers. "Retro quaint."

"It must be useful," says Dan. "I'm hopeless at remembering facts."

"It doesn't mean I'm super-brainy," I say. "But I can revise well for exams. I joined in January part way through last year but I caught up quickly. It helps."

"I bet it does. I could do with it now."

"I can't necessarily write a good essay or solve theorems. I can regurgitate information well, that's all."

Except that it's not all. I'm the mutant who

remembers *everything*.

"Which can be mistaken for genius," says Dan.

"I saw a TV series once which paraded quirky ten-year-olds in bow ties and velvet jackets and tested them," I say. "For the tiger parents it was all about hours of tuition, rote learning and memory testing so that they could wow the world with the correct spelling of 'tenesmus' and know pi to the nth place. That's not the same thing as genius."

"I guess for genius you need original thought," he says.

"Solving the antibiotic-resistance problem, showing the world in a new way," I say. "More than knowing a back road to Ashburton."

"I wouldn't say no to it, though." He slows down on a ridge. "Look at that view. You can see all the way to the coast. Beautiful."

"Where's home?" I ask.

"Not so far away. Cornwall. I grew up by the sea. You?"

"Suburbia: tarmac and wheelie bins."

"We'll have to go to the beach on our next trip. Get learning the route."

Next trip?

"I like having my very own satnav person." Dan

smiles over at me and I feel a flutter of excitement. Is this drop-dead gorgeous, sensitive, clever guy – with his own car, however ancient – coming on to me?

"Do you ever think if that memory part of your brain is so advanced maybe something else is less developed?" says Dan, wiping condensation off the windscreen. "Your sense of smell, drawing talent?"

I do think about that. I've read books and papers on it. And I've worked out exactly what I'm missing.

But to him I say: "I'm hopeless at dance. A complete klutz."

Dan laughs. "Yeah? So am I. We should go dancing sometime, memory girl."

10

Dum memor ipse mei
As long as I can remember who I am

Aeneid Book 4 – *Virgil*

I tried to shake him off but it turns out Dan's quite good company. Who'd have thought I could have fun in a tiny little Devonshire town? For a couple of hours I feel almost normal, my usual defences breaking down. I don't feel the pressure of the bad stuff rattling away at me from the shelves of my mind-library. I keep the Autobiography section locked as best I can. I don't know how, but Dan's able to potter about in charity shops as though they're the most interesting places he's ever been to. Maybe Cornwall's even more boring than here. He buys cassettes for the car while

I choose old board games. He tries on clothes from the seventies and I tease him we should match the Mini so I tie a bandana round my hair and put him in cool sunglasses and a beige jacket.

We get wistful looks from the old lady at the Devon Hospice shop who says we remind her of when she and her husband were young. Dan dances with her round the clothing rails to a Fleetwood Mac album, then when she needs a breather he switches to me.

"I said I'd take you dancing," he says, twirling me under his arm.

We pay for our stuff and the shop lady gives me a wink and says, "Your boyfriend's very handsome." And I don't correct her on either point. Dan makes things feel easy, normal.

He says we should pair up as a team for the hike and kits me out with thick socks and I buy a slab of Kendal Mint Cake as though we're proper walkers.

But just when I'm relaxing and enjoying myself for a change, Hanna butts in and ruins the moment. She was always good at that.

"You must miss Hanna," says Dan. "What was she like?"

Instantly a thousand images of her swoop before me. I blink hard but she doesn't go away. Dan's standing there, expecting a tearful reminiscence. How do I sum her up to someone who never knew her? What was the essence of her? Of any of us? "She loved fresh air," I say. "I was always shutting the windows and she'd open them again. This melancholic band called Silent Fjords was her favourite and she played them all the time." I see her, clear as anything, sitting on the bed, singing along. "She was uninhibited," I add. "Sitting around in only her pants, painting her toenails."

"I think I'd have liked her," says Dan. "Especially the pants behaviour."

"She was really beautiful but she couldn't see it herself." I remember her in that last week, peering in the mirror, popping pills. Asking my opinion. She didn't have to take it.

Dan hugs me to him, right there in the walking-boot section of Dart Outdoors, before I can react. "Sorry," he says, patting my back. "I shouldn't have asked."

No, he shouldn't have. Because now I'm seeing again in my head Hanna's parents clinging to each other when they came to collect the body. Remembering how I helped her dad pack away all her things while he tried so hard not to crumple in a heap. I hid some stuff. No grieving father wants to see the nitty-gritty of his daughter's contraceptive pills and medicine cabinet. How he *thanked* me for helping, being such a comfort to them, offered me a memento.

I blink again, refocusing on the boots displayed in front of us. I'll remember this instead: every stitch mark, every lace, every price. I'll concentrate on the smell of Dan, how strong his arms feel, how deep his voice is.

I did nothing wrong. Hanna was a fool. I pull back from Dan. "It's OK. It's good to remember," I say and falter a smile.

*

Dan's bought me a hot chocolate with extra marshmallows and whipped cream, and a madeleine cake to dunk. He softly talks to me about how he's lost someone before, how hard it is, how it's OK to feel sad. I feel I'm trapped in an edition of a touchy-feely show. "Maybe because it was sudden, there are things you feel you should've said to her or apologized for?" He takes my hand. "You can always talk to me – vicar's son and all that. We've only known each other a short time, but I feel I've known you for ages."

He's right, and I haven't had that before with anybody. But if he thinks I'm about to spill my innermost secrets to him, he's way off. I preferred him when he was dancing round the shop and distracting me from the memories. I don't want to list them all. He's expecting me to cry on his shoulder *right now*. "I'm sorry," I say. "I don't normally blub over people."

"Hey, what are second-hand jackets for, if not to wipe your nose on?"

But that's not what I meant at all. I meant I don't normally cry *about* people. I don't normally cry full stop. Professor Coleman and her techniques kind of knocked that out of me.

"Come and choose some snacks and a DVD," says Dan, pulling me up. "We could have a movie night."

We head down the High Street. He reaches for my hand but I shove it firmly in my pocket. We stop by the Ashburton Stores but I can't go in. It's a mini-market with CCTV. It's not worth the risk.

"You go on. I need to run a quick errand. Meet you by the clock tower." And before he can follow me I start walking, saying, "Don't get any chick-flick rubbish."

"Pretentious foreign films with subtitles only, I swear," he says.

The tiny post office/craft shop/tourist office smells of cats but it doesn't have a working camera. I do my banking here over the counter, withdrawing cash, checking my balance. It's always a relief that the money's still there. I've been careful, but even so. I didn't steal it – how can you steal it if nobody knows it's gone? And she shouldn't have had it in the first place. I reckoned Coleman owed me. I worked out an hourly rate for all the time I'd spent, and Mum had spent, on *her* research, on making her a big name in cognitive neuroscience, plus a healthy chunk for expenses to carry me through. And then I took a percentage of what she'd been paid – and what I saw she was going to be paid. The figures I found hidden in her documents. I'm not an expert on university research funding, but it's definitely not usual to be paid in wads of cash.

I flick through the postcards of Dartmoor made by local artists while I'm waiting, and spot a pack of five which includes the Haytor Rocks postcard that was put in my bag. They're just some cheap postcards, I tell myself. Nothing to get freaked about.

But then my eye is caught by the community noticeboard on my way out. Amid the car boot sales and the charity coffee mornings and the open-air pool hours, there's something new since last time. Something that chills me to the core: a printed flyer which I take down quickly and scrunch into a ball.

'MISSING – Freya Walsh. HAVE YOU SEEN THIS GIRL?'

There's a contact number. The name to call is Brett Young.

And the girl on the flyer is me.

*

I wait for Dan by the clock tower, holding the screwed-up flyer in my pocket, trying not to think about Brett. I can smell the exhaust and hear the purr and splutter of Uja before I see it. The horn toots.

Dan leans over and shoves open the passenger door. "Hey, you, want a lift in a classic car?"

I am genuinely pleased to see him. "Yes, but I'll settle for this heap of junk."

"But this 'heap of junk' has a minibar. Ta-da!" Dan smiles and opens the glovebox, showing me the pile of chocolate, crisps and cans. "Hop in. And to think you weren't keen on coming out with me today. Look at how much fun you're having now. Who would you have got to insult if you'd stayed behind?" He taps me on the knee and smirks. "Put on one of the new cassettes and navigate us home, Miss Google Maps."

I play the 'Classical Spectacular'. I focus my racing mind on listening for the beats. Breathe. Breathe. Don't panic. The photograph was grainy and two years old. I split the orchestra into different sections in my head, listening for each instrument. First the violins, then the violas, the cellos and the double bass. Breathe. I can feel the fear. Fear from seeing Brett's name again, and all the fear I've felt before. I'm flashing back, replaying, replaying.

Dan's whistling along, cheerful, carefree.

I listen for the brass section, isolate the tubas, the horns, the trumpets and the cornets. I'm remembering Brett. I can feel his hands on my arms, holding me until they bruise. Thinking *How far will he go?* Thinking *Surely he'll stop. Surely Coleman will stop it.* Wishing I was stronger.

The wind section. The bassoons, the oboes, the clarinets and flutes. Calm. Breathe.

Dan interrupts me and I open my eyes again. "Jess? Which way?"

I hear the timpani and can feel my pulse regularizing. "Straight on. Keep going."

I listen for the finale, the cadence at the end of the piece. An unfinished cadence. And my fingers tighten around the paper in my fist. They're looking for Freya.

They're looking for *me*.

11

A half-truth is a whole lie.

Yiddish proverb

Nobody at Dartmeet knows I'm called Freya. I did a professional job on my new identity. It's always better to steal one than start from scratch and it's best to choose something common, but not too common. So that rules out Smith and Jones. Wilson is in the top ten British surnames. And Jessica was in the top five names for girls across the years 2000 to 2005. And there are permutations to muddy the water: Jess, Jessica, Jessamy, Jessie (extra popular after *Toy Story*). Best not to be unusual if you want to fade into the background.

If Coleman is number one on my list of people to avoid, Brett Young is number two. When I left the Programme, I made it clear that I didn't want to be found. I take precautions, I stay silent and, so far as I know, they haven't looked. Until today.

Dan nudges me when we arrive back at Dartmeet. "Help me carry the gear to mine," he says. "Or do you want to meet me later?"

But after the shock of seeing my face on the flyer, I don't want to be on my own, in my room. I'd like a distraction this evening, a strong displacement activity. And, let's be honest, I fancy the pants off him. His arm brushes against mine as we take the bags out of the boot and I know he's feeling a spark there too.

We skip supper and the noise and company of the dining room and go to Dan's room in B-Block.

"Felix is away for the night at his parents'," he says. He nods over at the unmade bed. "His dad's fiftieth or something. So we won't be disturbed, you know, if…" Their room smells of Lynx and games kit. He shoves some books off his bed for me to sit down.

Dartmeet may be a progressive college but there are limits. When Lena Petrova was found in the swimming-pool showers with Benjamin in a compromising position they were both suspended for a week.

Benjamin didn't come back – his parents didn't want their son corrupted and moved him to a Quaker college in New Jersey.

Lena spent a week in the family apartment in Knightsbridge, supervised by the housekeeper, catching up on her shopping, but came back, promising to avoid 'certain situations' as Principal Barker put it.

What they really want is discretion and effective birth control because, let's face it, lock up a mixed bunch of sixteen- to eighteen-year-olds in an isolated community and you're going to have 'certain situations'. A few of the Americans have taken the virgin pledge at their previous high schools so they're no fun at all, hanging at the edge of parties like the morality police. Though I'm not the type to sleep around. Rejection replayed a thousand times over is tough. Until Ed, I hadn't really wanted to. And then, thanks to Hanna, I didn't get the opportunity to take the risk. But Dan…

"We can either go to the Common Room to watch the DVD, intense and subtitled as requested," says Dan, ineffectually pushing back his fringe. "And ask your friends along: Keira, Maya?"

"Or?" I say, looking straight into his eyes, feeling my heart go *boom boom* in my chest like we're stuck in a lame teen-magazine romance.

"Or…" He blushes in a completely charming, make-me-melt way. "Or stay here. And play games." He pulls Twister and Frustration from our shopping bags.

While he puts some vinyl on the turntable, I ponder whether I've misunderstood and he actually wants to play a board game, or whether there's an obvious innuendo at play and he assumes that I know exactly what he's talking about. Now I look silly because I'm not responding in the correct way, but then if I've got it wrong I don't want to act like an idiot. I tell myself the type of music he chooses will show which way the evening's panning out.

But then it's jazz. What the heck does that mean?

"You're still wearing my jacket," he says. "Better, you know, take it off."

That must be a sign, surely. I swallow and ease it off my shoulders, sensing Dan watching. Intently.

"Twister, then?" he says, managing to make it sound like a filthy idea. I spin the arrow and, before I know it, I'm definitely in one of Barker's 'certain situations'. Good. I desperately want to think and feel something else in my present, to be in the moment not in the accumulated past. I'd thought Coleman wasn't looking for me, that I'd left all that behind. I've got used to being Jess Wilson with the long blond hair and the sketchy past. I *am* Jess Wilson. I'm Jess Wilson making out with Dan. Gorgeous, funny Dan.

*

I wake up and take a moment to work out where I am. It's after midnight. I disentangle my limbs from Dan's, get fully dressed and step over the discarded Twister mat so I don't wake him. I haven't gone all considerate and thoughtful – I just don't want a conversation about what happened. Not that very much did – it was not a non-stop night of passion – it was fooling around and then falling asleep. But I don't want to see any regret on his face or disappointment or embarrassment. What was I even thinking? I've known him for, like, five whole minutes. A bad decision. When I'm stressed, that's what I do. Idiot.

I grab my swim stuff and slip into the pool. I want to clear my head, process the time with Dan and try to stop cringing with embarrassment. Length after length to make it better, more manageable. But I can't even concentrate on that, the Missing Person flyer keeps interrupting.

I take a long hot shower back in my own room. As I dry my hair, I check if the colour's fading. My dyed-blond hair covers my ears and masks the shape of my face, which makes it harder to spot me on CCTV. It's not that much of a change of appearance from the younger girl on the flyer with her shorter brown hair but as I can't grow a beard or undergo plastic surgery with no questions asked, it's the best I can do. That and show up in public images as little as possible. If Coleman is looking for me, she'll use the super-recognizers.

I tear up the flyer and flush it down the loo, watching it spiral away.

*

Dan takes the seat next to me at lunch. "Hey, you," he whispers, nudging my elbow in an overgrown schoolboy kind of way, which is what he is. He's grinning broadly. He may as well stand on a chair and make an announcement: "Jess and I fooled around together last night, people." Maya's gossip antennae are twitching away and Keira's mouth is open in an OMG shape already.

"This roast chicken is delicious," I say and Maya kicks me under the table.

"Shall we try out the route for Hanna's Hike this afternoon?" says Dan, looking only at me. "Or do you want to chill?"

Oh dear. This whole 'are we a couple?' type conversation is weird. I don't know what got into me last night. But I do know I don't want someone following me around like a puppy dog, acting like we're betrothed. I need to refocus on Coleman, Brett and my whole existence here.

"Or do you want to resume our board games? Maybe Frustration this time? Or not…" he whispers in my ear. Maya and Keira exchange knowing glances and raised eyebrows.

"I've got so much homework to do," I say, which everyone round the table knows is a lie this weekend. "And there's revision for the test in biology."

He looks hurt. Embarrassed. He knows the biology revision is not an issue for me. He knows I'm making excuses.

Keira's looking pleased, though. No doubt hoping to be first reserve, a shoulder to cry on for Dan. "I'd love some help sticking up the Hanna's Hike posters if you're free, Dan," she says, doing the full pouty smile, as I retreat from the room.

I've got bigger things to worry about than Keira.

When I get back to my room, there's a postcard of
Ryders Bridge wedged under the door handle.

HISTORY IS WHAT WE CHOOSE TO REMEMBER.

12

A mnemonist is a trained memorizer. All of us can benefit from an understanding of their techniques and exhibit an improvement in memory. But a true eidetiker isn't knowingly using those techniques. Their recall comes from a different place entirely.

Principles of Memory – *Professor A.E. Coleman*

I stay up late, pretending not to hear Dan knocking on my door. One postcard I can ignore as a lame joke, or put in the wrong bag, but now there's a second I can't dismiss it so easily. I work for hours, trying to find everything recent on Professor Andrea Coleman. I need to get up to speed. After all these months trying to shut them out of my thoughts, I have to think about her and Brett Young again. The deluge of information online is exhausting as my brain gets sucked into absorbing the hundreds of links. I read page after page, twisting Mum's pearl in my fingers.

I check Coleman's university website and see pictures of her smiling, receiving awards. Brett's still there, shown pointing at a shiny new scanner. He's written a moving piece on the spread of Alzheimer's in his own family, as though he cares about people and has an actual heart, which I know is completely false.

I look at science journals, newspapers, Facebook entries, reviews of her new book, just out: *Principles of Memory*. What is she up to? Is the flyer connected with the postcards? It's a jigsaw. I'm looking for all the pieces but I don't know yet what the full picture is behind the public veneer. In a way, I'm looking for missing pieces, the ones you don't see, the ones they need to hide. The lies.

Why are they trying to find me *now*, after all these months? I need to read her book. I eventually fall asleep propped up in bed, slumped over my laptop.

*

Today I've decided I'll be the model student, the model friend: I want no more drama. I say hello to everyone when I sit down at Maya's table. I pass Keira her pencil case and offer round my chewing gum without being asked. I even say a perky 'Good Morning' to Mr Desai as he hands back our essays on delegating memory.

I half-smile at Dan at the back of the class to make amends. He glances down. Then he glances at Keira.

"We're going to be using techniques in this workbook. Use it to make your own notes, create your own games and tools," says Mr Desai. He looks at me. I swear, he looks me straight in the eyes. "To improve your memory."

I flick through the book: *Work Your Memory*. Mind maps, number-rhyme, loci and peg systems, memory palaces, etc.

"Mnemosyne was the Greek goddess of memory, as those of you with the benefit of a classical education will know. We'll be making use of some mnemonics, or memory aids," says Mr Desai, handing out worksheets. "You'll be familiar already with some rhyming ones: *Thirty days hath September, April, June and November*, etc. But we can also use the first letter of each word to make a more memorable word: BIDMAS in maths or SOHCAHTOA in trigonometry. Or to make a new phrase. You all know the rainbow colours from Richard Of York Gave Battle In Vain, for example."

Mr Desai holds up the sheet. "So at the risk of our lesson turning into a round at a pub quiz, I want you to have a stab at these. There will be a prize for the best pair." He places a tub of Celebrations on the desk. Suddenly everyone is keen. You wouldn't think a bunch of teenagers could be so easily motivated by a small chocolate in a shiny wrapper but there's a flurry of activity. I scan his list:

Sergeant Major Hates Eating Onions

FACE

All Cows Eat Grass

Every Good Boy Deserves Fun

Good Boys Deserve Fun Always

Father Christmas Gave Dad An Electric Blanket

My Very Easy Method Just Speeds Up Naming Planets

How I want a drink, alcoholic of course, after the heavy chapters involving quantum mechanics

Did Mary Ever Visit Brighton Beach?

I'm saddled with Maya, who turns out to be more useful than I thought as she has Grade 7 piano and whizzes through the music-reading ones.

"*FACE* and *All Cows Eat Grass*. You must have learned the recorder, right?" she says, sketching out a set of music staves.

"I gave up," I say. "I was terrible."

"In the treble clef – the higher notes – *FACE* gives you the names of the notes in the spaces between the lines. *All Cows Eat Grass* gives the notes between the lines on the bass clef – the lower notes." She fills in the letter names. "Now for the notes on the lines: *Every Good Boy Deserves Fun* are the notes in the treble clef then *Good Boys Deserve Fun Always* are the notes in the bass clef. My music teacher taught me *Good Boys Don't Fool Around.* There are loads of ruder versions.

"Then *Father Christmas Gave Dad An Electric Blanket* is the order in which sharps are entered in the key signature like this. F sharp, C sharp etc." She adds seven sharps to the lines of music. "Easy if you know how. I guess I have a better memory than I thought."

She lowers her voice to a whisper. "I was pretty surprised about you and Danny Boy," she says.

"There is no me and Danny Boy," I say, picking up the sheet again. It's none of her business. She is not my best buddy, whatever she likes to pretend. She is not Hanna. What she really means, she and her effortless beauty, is that Dan is out of my league.

"Think about what makes a phrase memorable and what makes it work for you," says Mr Desai, "as your homework will be to design some of your own to help with your revision in other subjects."

Everyone agrees *My Very Easy Method Just Speeds Up Naming Planets* works best because it tells you what it's about; the new phrase relates to the original meaning. I make an educated guess that *Sergeant Major Hates Eating Onions* lists the Great Lakes in the US, west-to-east, of Lake Superior, Michigan, Huron, Erie and Ontario.

"*How I want a drink, alcoholic of course, after the heavy chapters involving quantum mechanics* is a code for pi in maths," I say. "The number of letters in each word match the digits of pi."

"Say what?" says Maya.

"The word 'How' has three letters, then 'I' has one, 'want' has four letters. It's basically a substitution code so 3.1415926535979, etc."

The only one we don't get is *Did Mary Ever Visit Brighton Beach?* – it turns out to be the order of hereditary titles, which I will never need again. If you were in a Jane Austen novel it could come in handy when selecting a husband. Apparently a Duke's better than a Marquis, who beats an Earl, then a Viscount, Baron and lastly a Baronet.

Maya's thrilled when we're the joint winners and get to split the chocolates.

"Well spotted for the pi one. There are a few alternatives for this to give even more digits," says Mr Desai. "And take a look at the number-rhyme system in the book which can help with learning long numbers."

"So it's all a trick?" says Maya, already chewing a gooey chocolate.

"I prefer to say technique," says Mr Desai.

"Though it's odd that to remember one thing you have to remember something else as well," says Maya.

"I guess some things are easier to remember than others," I say.

"The memory men who appear on stage are full of these tricks, then?" says Maya.

"It's an illusion, like the magician who saws a lady in half," says Keira.

"So you don't believe that some people have an innate ability, a power, Mr Desai?" asks Dan, glancing at me.

"I do believe that. Some people have an amazing memory – maybe they use basic mnemonics as part of their natural brain function, without even being aware of it." Mr Desai lingers at our table, peering at our notes again.

If I were a paranoid person, which let's face it, I am, I would wonder what this whole elaborate memory project is all about. I know memory is on the TOK syllabus – I'd been looking forward to hearing Ms Mac stutter her way through it – but I can't shake the feeling that Mr Desai is testing us. Is he testing *me*?

As soon as the bell goes I want to get out of there. I don't want Mr Desai asking me any more questions, plus I don't want Dan coming over and expecting me to behave in a certain way and Maya and Keira staring like it's impossible anyone could be interested in me. I ignore the social niceties of waiting for the others and barge my way towards the door.

"Hey!" says Dan, as my bag catches him on the arm. "Watch where you're going."

"Sorry," I say. "I'm in a rush."

"To get away from me?"

"No! I, er…"

"It's pretty shitty of you – ignoring me since Saturday. If I did that to a girl, you'd say I was a complete thoughtless jerk." Dan's face looks like a PSHE lesson: Guys have feelings too. This whole exchange is feeling like a low-budget educational video we're shown to get the message.

He's right of course that I've behaved badly. But then I'm messed up. I'm a complete emotional wreck. Part of me wants to tell him this. Tell him that sometimes I'm tired of being me. I ran away from the Programme but it's harder to run away from myself.

"I don't want any complications at the moment,"

I say, which sounds lame, even as I'm saying it. The sort of cowardly line that I'd go nuts about if anyone said it to me. "I've got a lot on."

As I leave, he says under his breath: "What? Two pieces of homework and a secret swim session?"

Stuff him. I've got enough to worry about and I do have a lot on. I stop at the Hanna shrine. It needs some major tidying after all the rain today. I tip out the jars of soggy tea lights and relight them. The laminated photo of her has seen better days. I should replace it. I can see Dr Harrison out of the corner of my eye. He's watching me from his doorway. No doubt he'll be writing it all down in his case notes. He'll be working through the five stages of grief with me again, giving me another leaflet; as if I can't remember the last one.

If anything happened to me, would I get any of the attention Hanna's had? There'd be no relatives dashing here with hankies. Would Barker even find out who I really am? I certainly wouldn't want a commemorative hike in my honour or a mawkish church service. Maybe I should leave instructions. But who would care?

I make my way to the office for a word with the administrator. She's bashing away at the keyboard as though it's offended her. I wait patiently until she's ready to acknowledge me. In her own time she stops and looks over her glasses at me. "Do you want to see the Principal?"

"Actually, I was hoping I could send a card to Ms Mac," I say. "To wish her a speedy recovery. Should I give it to you?"

"Ms Mac isn't ill."

"But I thought that was why she wasn't here and we had Mr Desai on supply," I say, innocence personified.

"No, no. A last-minute sabbatical." She looks around, checking the door to Principal Barker's office is still shut and lowers her voice. "She's off on a Caribbean cruise. Funny sort of sabbatical. Not many opportunities for Theory of Knowledge doing the limbo with a rum punch in one hand. But there we are. Some of us have a proper job to do."

So Ms Mac isn't ill. Then why was she taken off the timetable unexpectedly like that? So that Mr Desai could fulfil a burning ambition to teach us lot? At the same time as I start to get weird messages. They say that thirty-four per cent of paranoid delusionals have a legitimate basis for their paranoia. I'm beginning to think I'm in the thirty-four per cent.

In fact, I know I am. Because when I walk into the

college library I see *Principles of Memory* by Professor A.E. Coleman propped up on the *New Books* shelf. There's a reservation slip poking out of the top: '*Reserved for Jess Wilson*'.

13

Patients exhibiting hyperthymesia have difficulty overcoming the mental strain of bad memories and constantly living in the past. The rest of us have an inbuilt survival mechanism: the ability to forget.

Principles of Memory – *Professor A.E. Coleman*

"You haven't got a poster up for Hanna's Hike," says Maya. She pulls one out of her bag and reorganizes my noticeboard to make room for it. She's tagged along back to my room after supper to show me the Hanna's Hike T-shirt design, as if I care, and generally ruin my evening.

"Only *I'm* going to see it in here, and I know about it, don't I? I'm on the committee." I slump into the chair and kick off my shoes.

"Ah, but from what I hear, you might not be the only person in here at nights lately. Care to spill?"

She looks expectantly at me, her eyebrows raised and a conspiratorial smile on her lips. "Well? The delectable Dan? Things are moving quickly. I don't want you to get hurt."

Not again. Can Maya be any more annoying? Pretending to be concerned when she just wants the gossip. Now she's in here, it's going to be hard to get her out. I may have to play the Hanna-grief card. Again.

"What's this?" Maya takes something from my noticeboard. "Is it your phrase for Mr Desai?" It's a postcard of Buckfast Abbey from the pack on sale at the post office. A new one. I can feel the *thud*, *thud* of my heart. The card has a line printed in familiar black handwriting:

BODIES ESPECIALLY AFTER DEATH GO COLD, FREYA

"Yuk! Couldn't you come up with a less grisly mnemonic?" asks Maya. "It's the order of flats in music, B flat, E flat, etc., right? I think the original one's nicer. *Blanket Explodes And Dad Gets Cold Feet.*"

My actual name. Calm down, it's just a mnemonic. Like choosing Richard for red in the rainbow colours. Freya for the note F. Is it just a coincidence?

Maya has moved on to picking up the books on my bedside table. "Blimey. This isn't light reading, is it?

Principles of Memory."

"It's for biology," I lie, taking it off her. "I'm doing an extended project on the brain." Why's she picking up *that* book? Did she plant the postcard herself? Is all this friendliness an act, and she's reporting back to Coleman?

Bodies Especially After Death Go Cold, Freya.

I saw Hanna's smashed-up brain and body. When it was still warm to the touch. Before it was cold. I know because I touched her hand. I held her hand. Until Barker prised me off after they'd checked her for vital signs. Harrison was flapping and he threw up at the sight of her. He's got medical training for Christ's sake. Or so he claims. The chaplain was more use. She kneeled beside me and was so calm. She held her cross with one hand and said, "Let God take her now, Jess." Just like that. But God didn't take her. The paramedics took her – the main bit of her. The blood and flesh and brain on the cobbles were photographed and looked at and eventually washed off with a pressure hose by the groundsman. As if he was cleaning off the decking by the Common Room. Tiny, microscopic elements of Hanna splashed against the walls of A-Block and all around the quad, swirling down the drains.

"Jess?"

I look at Maya. What was she saying? Order. Get your head in order.

"So can I borrow it?" She's holding up the bandana from the charity shop. "It's so retro."

"Sure." I don't want it any more. It reminds me of old clothes and the dead people they belonged to and dancing round a stack of rails before I got back to reality.

"What do you think?" Maya shows me a picture of a lime-green T-shirt with a hiking-boot design containing black lettering: 'Hanna's Hike. Walking together to remember.' "I thought we could repeat it every year," she says. "I mean, I know *we*'ll have left by the summer but some people who knew her have got another year and we could come back for it. An annual reunion."

This hike idea is bad enough once, but twice, three times? An annual event in the school calendar? Piling memory upon memory of Hanna. These people have the ability to forget and yet they want to keep remembering. I don't get it.

"The design's great," I say. Maya's good at art, much better than me. I know what I want to draw but I don't seem able to communicate that to my hand. Coleman took me to an exhibition by an autistic artist who can draw detailed cityscapes from memory. A true photographic memory coupled with the artistic talent to reproduce it. Something I could never do.

"If you're sure you're OK with the T-shirts?" she asks again. She's so needy. 'I'll order them now."

"Yes, good idea," I say, sensing a chance to wrap this up and get her out of here. All I can focus on is the postcard, as if it's written in ten-foot-high characters on a billboard, surrounded by flashing lights and arrows.

Bodies Especially After Death Go Cold, Freya.

After Maya leaves, I lock the door and wedge the desk chair up under the handle. I sit on my bed, hugging my knees, staring at the door, jumping at any footsteps in the corridor.

Someone has been in my room. Someone wants to creep me out.

And it's working.

14

Better by far you should forget and smile
Than that you should remember and be sad
                          'Remember' – Christina Rossetti

The mnemonic message is still staring at me from the noticeboard in the morning. I didn't sleep well, half-listening for an intruder. Trying not to freak out. Lena didn't help by scaring me half to death fumbling with my lock at three a.m., instead of her own one on the floor above.

I look again at all the cards. The one I found at the shrine addressed to Hanna is plainly different from the ones given directly to me. Smart envelope, crisp cream card, sprawling cursive handwriting. I recall the creepy message signed *HCC* in the Book of Condolence and try to compare the styles in my head. One is a slanting italic written with an ink pen, one was written with the biro provided by the chaplain. They could be written by the same person in different ways, but then again... The bottom line is I can't tell.

I turn my attention to the postcards. Sent by somebody working their way through the pack of five, with neat, printed handwriting. Purchased in town, hand-delivered secretly, to my own room. Someone who can come and go unchallenged at college. Students here don't tend to lock their doors, especially as many rooms are shared. It's not that sort of place. 'Holistic, caring, international.' There's security at the porters' lodge at the gatehouse and a keypad at each accommodation block. But it'd be easy to walk in behind someone else, or watch them type the code. Could it be one of my so-called friends? Are Keira and Maya not as dopey as they seem? Have they been playing with my emotions all this time? Or is new-boy Dan too good to be true? And what about Mr Desai and his memory lessons? If Coleman's doing it and knows I'm here, why is she putting up Missing Person fliers? She and Brett always liked to play games, but with a purpose. Is this them? I'm sick of all the questions with no answers. I curl up on the bed.

Bodies Especially After Death Go Cold, Freya is the freakiest message yet. It refers to my past, *Freya's* past. I've tried so hard to leave it all behind.

Because Hanna's wasn't the first dead body I'd seen. The first one was my mum's.

I put what happened to Mum in the deepest locked room in the deepest basement of my mind-library. It has a different feel to my other memories – blurrier, harder to watch. Even so, it's all too easy for it to seep out and be replayed in multicoloured detail over and over. I put my hands over my eyes but I know it doesn't make a difference. I can still *see* it. I've replayed that scene a thousand times under lab conditions, describing it again and again. I *see* it every day. Mum talking with Coleman, stepping into the road. There was nothing the elderly driver could do. It was a red Range Rover. It matched Mum's lipstick.

At first I didn't want to see Mum's body in the hospital. The accident was bad enough to witness. I didn't want another terrible memory that would last forever. Coleman broke the news that they couldn't save her then she took me back to her smart house in Kensington. Even Brett was nice to me, helping me upstairs and laying me on the bed like an invalid. They gave me something to help me sleep.

When I woke, I asked to see Mum's body. Coleman was adamant it was a bad idea, too traumatizing. "Don't put yourself through it, Freya," she'd said. "You don't want to remember her forever as a broken body on a hospital slab. Think of her as she was, with her fashionable clothes and her beautiful hair and her lipstick."

But I insisted. I didn't want to think of Mum alone, on a pull-out drawer in a fridge in the hospital basement somewhere. I've seen the movies. We rowed about it. I said if I couldn't see her one last time, I'd walk out of the house and go to the hospital and scream in the foyer until someone took me to her. Coleman said she'd pull some strings, arrange something at the hospital.

She drove us there the next day. We took the lift from the underground car park. Coleman held my hand tightly, which was unlike her, but I guess even she has a heart at times. She took me down a grey corridor through double fire doors clicking shut behind us. Her lanyard and security card were magic keys opening locked doors while she walked briskly on, dragging me with her.

I was expecting a chapel, called something dumb to make you feel better like the Chapel of Eternal Rest or the Chapel of Sweet Remembrance. But it turned out to be a depressing grey room with a chair and a window. A window into another, smaller, depressing grey room. Mum was lying in there. I could see her through the glass. I hadn't seen a dead body, a dead *person* before. If you stare at them long enough you can swear they're breathing, see things when there's nothing to see. She had a sheet over her, pulled up to her chin, as though someone had tucked her in for the night. Although no one sleeps like that, do they? Fully clothed and lying flat on their back on a cold trolley.

"I should kiss her goodbye," I said, but Coleman held my hand firmly on this side of the wall.

"It's not allowed now, dear. You're too late." She gave me a tissue and a stilted hug.

I stared at Mum for a while. I wanted to smash through the glass and stroke her cheek, reach through and brush her hair because it wasn't how she used to do it. The parting was all wrong. I wiped at the glass with my sleeve where it was misty but the moisture was on the other side. I didn't want the glass to be dirty, which was stupid, because it's not like she'd have noticed.

And then Coleman led me away.

I couldn't face a church funeral. Mum wasn't a

believer and we have no other family. Coleman organized the cremation and then we scattered the ashes during a boat trip on the Thames. Surreptitiously of course. You're not allowed to chuck dead people into the river or public spaces, whatever state they're in.

I was a complete mess. Numb and broken.

Coleman sorted out my life, took over. My brain went into overdrive. It was a set of dominoes – each memory tumbled into another and another. I moved permanently into her house. Brett settled up our outstanding rent, brought the rest of my things, boxed up my mum's, and paid for a storage unit. Her life in thirty cardboard boxes. I only kept the necklace with me, for sentimental reasons. A talisman. I touch the pearl now, pulling it from side to side along the chain.

Coleman put me on to the next stage of the Programme so we could work through the trauma together, which seemed to be incessantly reliving the accident. I was hyper at times, comatose at others. She gave me talking therapy, hypnosis, something to help me sleep; the whole box of tricks.

I didn't scatter all of Mum into the Thames – I keep a handful in a box in my trunk. I go and get it now and then and pat the lid. When I go abroad, I'll take her with me. She always wanted to go to New York.

15

When falsehood can look so like the truth…

Frankenstein – *Mary Shelley*

I went swimming last night. Forty lengths but it didn't work as well as usual to relax me. I was still wound up tight like a spring when I finished. I had a nagging fear that someone might be watching me from the shadows outside. I used to revel in the solitude of the pool 'after hours' but found myself wishing Dan would appear again. An attentive bodyguard could be just what I need. *If* I can trust him. But we haven't spoken since the incident in Mr Desai's class and Keira's probably launched an offensive by now to get her claws into him.

I pick up *Principles of Memory*. Coleman's photo smiles out at me from the cover. I normally skip the dedication page in books – 'To my sister Mary-Lou who's always been there for me', 'For my own little pussy cat, Tibbles' – that sort of schmaltzy nonsense. But Coleman's book has:

'*For F.*

Gone but not forgotten'

Like a gravestone inscription. Like *my* gravestone inscription. Nice.

I'm reading at a slower rate than usual, making sure I fully understand all she says. I can hear her plummy voice in my head as I read the words. There are disguised references to me throughout and plenty of chapters on her pet topic of treating post-traumatic stress disorder. She talks about preventing bad memories from embedding by using reconsolidation therapies, though she's vague on the detail. There's no mention of her unorthodox techniques. But there is a passing mention of personality change: '*These techniques to limit the storage of disturbing memories are not without side effects and consequences in the personality and behaviour of the subject.*' Is that what she observed in me? Has she made me vengeful and mean and…?

I shudder as I recall Hanna. In our old room in

A-Block, she'd sniffed at the dodgy diet drink she'd made up and wrinkled her pretty little nose. I didn't stop her. I was glad her skin was getting spotty and her cheeks pinched. I was glad she was throwing up, becoming so withdrawn. I'd egged her on, played on her insecurities. And so she took a sip. And another.

I stare back down at Coleman's book and read on. *'Further, the need to employ such techniques as spatial displacement quickly may well be impractical in a military or emergency-service setting. The whole field requires extensive research which, given the need for a stressful or traumatic incident to occur, is difficult to reproduce in the laboratory setting.'* It certainly is. She must have thanked her lucky stars when Mum's accident happened. A traumatized teenager to study, on a plate. I plough through the appendices of references too. The Programme isn't mentioned by name at all in the entire book. A whole set of facts missing, an untold story. So that's the missing jigsaw piece − literally erased from history.

I close the book and talk to her photo on the dust jacket. "No one outside the Programme knows about it, do they, Prof? It's your dirty little secret. But I know. Is *that* why you're looking for me? To make sure I stay quiet about it? And it's not fair that you're off publishing bestsellers and heading up a university department while I'm being scared by flyers and postcard messages." I trace the outline of her face: the dark hair in a bob, the smug smile. I go round and round, my fingernails digging in deeper and deeper, scratching into the cover.

I was brought up in a home that was full of sweet little mottos on fridge magnets. Mum collected them from service stations and tat shops at touristy hellholes like Cheddar Gorge. 'Don't get mad, get even', 'Revenge is a dish best served cold'. You get the idea. The time has come for Coleman to know that *I'm* watching *her*. I need actual proof of what she did to me on the Programme so I'm not dismissed as a disturbed teenager with a score to settle when I spill the beans. I'm going to find out the full extent of what she's hiding about the Programme. She should have let me be because now, one day soon, she's going to pay.

*

I have a free period late afternoon and hurry out of biology, before anyone can ask me where I'm going. I sign out and grab my coat for the long walk down the drive to the bus stop. It's a crisp, blue-sky day but the sun's already starting to tip towards dusk. I know exactly what I want to buy. I can play at sending messages too.

I select a book at the bookshop in Ashburton and write an inscription. The perfect, thoughtful gift – apt, erudite and rather Victorian Gothic: *Frankenstein* by Mary Shelley.

I sign it: *To the Prof*
Forever in my thoughts,
Your very own monster

The assistant gift wraps it for me – brown-paper parcel, tied up with string and a wax seal. I pay him extra to post it tomorrow when he's up in London at a book fair. I know the delivery address. I lived there for months after all. "It's a surprise for someone – a game we play," I say. "I don't want them to see a Devon postcode. That would ruin the fun."

"I'm all for games," he says. "What is life if not for playing?"

"Exactly so," I say.

Game on.

16

Try the following memory exercise: Read each word once. Close the book and write down as many as you can remember:

beach	*watch*
jumper	*camera*
surfboard	*smile*

Work Your Memory

I hurry back down Ashburton High Street in the dark, not wanting to miss the last bus back to school. I feel lighter already for doing something back at Coleman. 'Don't get mad, get even' really works. Mum's fridge magnet told the truth. I'm even humming. If I hum loud enough maybe I'll shut out all the memories of Coleman that are trying to gatecrash my good mood, memories of all the procedures and tests she put me through. The EEGs, the CT, MRI and PET scans. Testing, testing.

I hope Coleman gets a dose of sleepless nights and anxiety when she opens up her parcel, wondering where I am and whether I'm going to blow the whistle on how she really operates.

Out of the corner of my eye, I notice a vehicle slowing behind me. I look sideways at the reflection in the shop windows but I'm dazzled by the full-beam headlights. My heart rate quickens and I look for a shop to run into as it draws close.

Now I can see it properly. It's orange and a Mini and a pile of crap. It's Dan in Uja.

"You can get arrested for picking up girls like this," I say. "It's called kerb-crawling. And you a vicar's son too."

"Hop in quickly then before the cops arrive." He pushes open the passenger door for me and I get in.

"Fancy seeing you here," he says. "You're no longer avoiding me, then?"

He doesn't show any sign of driving off. It seems a heart to heart is the price to pay for the lift. "After you said I was a complete jerk, you mean," I say.

"You said I was a complication."

"Yeah, well, you're a complication who's offering me a lift home in the dark and cold," I say. "Though I guess I'm still a jerk, which is worse."

Dan laughs. "I may have overreacted at the time. And at least our first row is out of the way. Lucky

I'm the forgiving type."

"I'm not always good with how other people are feeling," I say. But I note his comment about the first argument, as though we're a couple, an actual boyfriend-girlfriend. He seems sincere, but... The car's slowly misted up with our breath and I wipe at the windscreen with his car cloth. "We're on a double yellow. You'd better move."

He reaches over and kisses me. Slowly. "What do you think I'm feeling now?" He kisses me again.

It's as physical as you can get with two people wearing seat belts strapped in separate seats. I'm melting. I've missed him. I've missed feeling like this, a surge of emotions taking me over, stopping my brain from whirling through the past. He helps me live in the present. Should I give us a go? Prove Maya wrong?

"See, it's not so hard to work me out." He makes to kiss me again, his hand travelling up my leg, but I'm worried about the woman who's stopped in front of the car. I swear she's peering in at us.

"We're in a car with windows by a street lamp. We're not invisible."

"You win, Little Miss Prudish." Dan puts the car into gear and flicks the indicators. "I'm glad we sorted things out," he says as he pulls away.

"I'm not one of those girls who likes PDAs all the time – especially at college," I say. "I don't want to be gossiped about."

"Understood. I won't ask you in public to play Twister again," he says. "Or Frustration. My mistake."

"I can't stand it when you're trying to talk to someone and their boyfriend's draped all over them, as if they're *wearing* him and he owns them. And the girl's trying to talk and his tongue is halfway down her throat."

"Yuk. Agreed. I will never do that," says Dan.

"And no his and hers teddy bears with messages on their jumpers?"

"Absolutely not."

"Nothing," I say. "I mean absolutely nothing on social media."

"OK. But you can't make any more rude comments about Uja," he says. "Or give me anything heart-shaped."

"Agreed. And not the G word or the B word."

"Dan and Jess?"

"Jess and Dan," I say.

Maybe it *is* possible to drive around in my 'boyfriend's' car and pretend to be normal. We'll watch movies and stress about exams and uni applications and spend our holidays surfing in Cornwall. I'll work on ways to forget, to recall things only when I want to.

"You drive a hard bargain but we are now officially… What's an acceptable term for you?" he says. "An item, a couple, going out, mutually exclusive, *lovers*?"

I like the smile on his lips and in his eyes. And I know how much I want to resume what we started. Even though I know it could end badly – it's *bound* to end badly – I find myself saying: "Just us. Just Jess and Dan."

17

You keep a little piece of me
You must be missing me, missing me already
                    'Missing Me Already' – Silent Fjords

"The loci or journey system," says Mr Desai. "A method used since Ancient Roman times. Pick a route you know very well. Walking through the college, for instance. Close your eyes and proceed up the drive, pass through the gatehouse arch, waving at the porter on duty, go up towards the chapel courtyard with the oak tree in the middle and the iron seat, Mandela Lodge is on your left-hand side – keep your eyes closed please, Miss Petrova – and you're turning into the cloister towards the chapel doors. Enter the chapel, walk up the aisle and take a seat on the front pew.

That's far enough for now."

He shows us a film on the whiteboard of all we've 'walked' in our heads, so we can soak up any details we've missed. "The route must be so familiar to you that you need no effort to remember it. Then you can attach items you wish to remember at the locations, or loci, of your route. You can add more familiar buildings as needed, creating whole 'memory palaces'. I myself am particularly fond of using the campus of the university where I had a research job in London. It's forever etched on my mind."

"Do you do all this?" asks Dan when no one else can hear us.

"Not exactly. It's more of a film that I choose to watch."

"Press play."

"Fast-forward or rewind. But all done in a nanosecond."

"Pay attention please, Jess and Dan," continues Mr Desai. "Concentration is the key to success. Now I shall demonstrate how we use that journey to place things to remember. Let's take the Christmas song 'The Twelve Days of Christmas'. As you enter the school grounds, you eat a pear from the pear tree but get pecked by the partridge roosting there. You pass a dovecote with two turtles sticking their scrawny necks out of the openings to signify the two turtle doves. Further along the drive you say *Bonjour* to three French hens riding bicycles with onions round their necks." He continues working his way through "The Twelve Days of Christmas" until he has placed twelve drummers drumming along the altar table in the chapel.

"Now take a piece of paper, and write out the song for me, using those vivid images we have located along the route."

I play along, even though my brain does this kind of thing naturally. I don't need to make up such vivid images. I look at my classmates, chattering excitedly about remembering a list of only twelve items. I wish I could forget, like them. They really don't realize how lucky they are.

Next, Mr Desai places a pile of sheets on each table. "Some of you will have poems, or passages of prose, some lists of historical dates and events. Apply the techniques we've been learning. Play with them, use whichever methods work for you. I expect you all to be word-perfect next lesson. And to show you the benefits of pushing your brain to work harder, I have printed these off in unusual, unfamiliar fonts. In working harder to process the text, you'll be surprised that the information will be better retained."

Keira dives in to get first pick. She gives me Shakespeare's 'Sonnet 30' written in twirly Blackadder font. All Gothic mourning and misery. Could Keira have written in the condolence book or sent the mourning card? I peer sideways at her notes, trying to examine her writing. But the notes are quickly taken: messy, abbreviated, inconclusive.

"I think my memory's getting better with all this," says Maya. "I got full marks on my French vocab test for the first time ever."

"And me," says Dan. "There's some good stuff in that memory workbook he gave us – the number-rhyme system and the mind maps. At this rate, we're going to be a whole class full of memory boffins. We'll be able to enter the World Memory Championships."

"What's the point, though, in being able to learn pages of binary numbers or to memorize a pack of cards in less than a minute?" asks Keira.

"Because it's cool. Those memory geeks get mobbed, I mean *mobbed* by all the Chinese and Malaysian chicks. Like a world-famous sportsman," says Makoto. "I watched some of the championships on YouTube last night."

"You could play blackjack in Las Vegas," says Lena. "You can work out your odds because you remember all the cards that have already been played. As long as the casino doesn't realize you're card-counting, you can become a millionaire."

"They would realize if you'd won the World Memory Championships," says Makoto.

"So then you have to choose between hot girls and the money. Tough choice," says Dan.

"You get a commemorative T-shirt too," says Makoto.

"You'd love it then, Maya," I say.

"Ha ha. Hilarious," she says, sticking up one finger.

"And did they look happy?" I ask. "The people competing, did they look happy?"

"Happy? They were ecstatic when they won, yeah." Makoto looks at me like I'm a weirdo for asking.

"Were you not listening to the part about the hot girls and the money?" asks Dan. "There are a lot of hot girls involved with memory feats." He smiles at me and nudges my leg under the desk with his foot.

*

I make my way to Mandela Lodge after TOK. I may as well move in for all the time I have to waste here. I can't be the only freak show in town in need of counselling. I'm regretting the deal I struck with Barker of extra sessions.

"I have a gift for you today," says Dr Harrison. "A special gift that I think will help." He produces a large gift bag from behind his armchair.

"Ooh, a present," I say, briefly interested. He hasn't given me anything better than a leaflet before.

I pull out a cardboard box from the bag; larger than a shoebox, decorated with pink roses and butterflies. It's hideous. If I were, like, eighty-two, I'd keep my knitting patterns in it.

"It's a memory box," he says.

"Er, thanks," I say. I open it but it's completely empty. I place it on the coffee table between us.

"A memory box helps when you've lost someone," he says. "Select a few items which remind you of Hanna, a photograph or two, and place them in here. Maybe write her a letter saying how you feel."

He has no idea. My whole head is a memory box.

"It helps to crystallize how you felt about the deceased, what they meant to you." He positions the box of tissues nearer to me, as though he's expecting an outpouring of tears over his cardboard box. "And as we move forward, you can compartmentalize your grief, looking in the box at certain times, say, birthdays or anniversaries," he carries on. "It's OK not to remember all the time. Grief doesn't have to overwhelm you." His usual non-stop stream of platitudes.

I never let grief overwhelm me. Not again. Not now. And certainly not over Hanna.

He sips at his tea then smiles at me smugly like he's come up with something amazing such as a cure for cancer or the answer to all my problems, not handed me an ugly box. "So let's talk through possible items to include, objects which sum up your friend?"

How do you sum someone up and cram them in a shoebox? I don't want to play this game with him, but he started it. I take the only chocolate biscuit on the plate and nibble it slowly to stretch out the time and look like I'm thinking really hard about what could go in there. The clock hands tick round. I like to build the suspense. "I have something in mind, though it's not what you'd call a sentimental item."

"If it has meaning or resonance for you, then of course it counts as a sentimental item." He smiles benignly.

"I've got some of her pills – like her contraceptive pills," I say. "I suppose that sums up a certain aspect of her character."

Dr Harrison splutters on his herbal tea. He's staring at me like I'm a terrible human being, which I am.

"I'm not going to take any of them," I say. I don't want him to think I'm going to overdose on all her different medications. "I also have a pen pot," I say, backtracking. "But I use it. It's on my desk, not shut away in a box." OK, so *she* didn't actually give it to me. Her dad said I could choose one thing from the box of sorry bits and pieces we gathered together when we cleared out the room. I thought he was going to cry, right there, so I did what was expected and picked the pen pot, which I now have to keep on my desk forever.

The memory box sits accusingly still, waiting for a normal item. I wish I *could* shove Hanna into a tacky box decorated with roses and butterflies and shut the lid on her. I wish I could only remember her when I choose to peek inside, rather than these constant intrusions into my head.

"Do you want me to put the pen pot in there, then?" I ask him, thinking this might be a good solution all round as I wouldn't have to look at it again.

"Session over for today," says Dr Harrison. He stands and clears the cups. They clatter together as he carries the tray to the sink. He keeps his back turned, washing up, as I gather my stuff and go.

I'm relieved, even though I sense he's disappointed with the reaction to his rubbish gift. I thought I had twenty minutes left of this claptrap. Another visit over but as usual I don't feel any better.

18

Play the game: Jess packed a one-eyed teddy, a pendant, a wooden box, an envelope of old photos…

Work Your Memory

Dan and I are hanging out in my room for the evening, pretending to do homework. I need to chill after my session with Harrison. But Dan has no attention span tonight. He keeps walking around and picking things up and putting them down, slightly out of place.

"I've finally worked out what's strange about your room," he says. "You haven't got any photos up. Not one."

I look at the bare walls and clear surfaces. A timetable and homework schedule are pinned neatly to the noticeboard, next to the Hanna's Hike poster.

"I moved rooms, so…"

"You must have some photos on your phone of friends and family." He goes to pick it up but I reach it first myself and put it in my pocket.

"No, not really. I don't need to look at a photo to think about someone."

"Most girls have knick-knacks, teddies, bracelets and earrings, a whole board of selfies with their friends…"

It sounds as though he's been in a lot of girls' bedrooms. Probably more than I've been in. I have a pang of jealousy.

"So where are you hiding your Hello Kitty pyjama case and your Sylvanian Families collection?" he asks.

"Seriously? Do I look as if I ever played with a Sylvanian Families treehouse?"

He opens the wardrobe doors and looks on the shelves.

I don't want anyone going through my stuff. I need to stop this. I take a breath and say more quietly, "When you've never met your dad, and your mum dies, you don't have a massive family portrait to put above the fireplace. We don't all live in your perfect world at the vicarage."

Dan looks horrified. "I didn't mean… Your mum? I'm so sorry. I had no idea." His cheeks are glowing red.

"I don't tell everyone. I don't want people feeling sorry for me. It's nobody's business."

"No, of course. However you want to play it." He sits on the floor next to me and puts his arm round my shoulders and kisses my cheek. "Your room's great as it is," he says. "Honest."

"It's barer now. Hanna was the one big on clutter. That pen pot was hers," I say, pointing at the desk.

"And this." Dan pulls at the chunky jumper I'm wearing.

"Yes, and her make-up bag that she was always precious about. It's under the bed, not on display or anything. *That* would be weird. Satisfied?"

"I'm an idiot," he says, gently kissing my forehead. I can feel my annoyance with him melting away. I want to trust him, I do.

"I do have a few photos of Mum, if you ask nicely," I say.

"I'd love to see them. Please." He kisses me again.

I hesitate for a moment when I go to get the key from the box of tampons in the bathroom. Part of me wants to share at least something of my real self, and part of me's holding back, being paranoid and stupid. I look at myself in the mirror, hoping for an answer.

"Jess?" He's knocking gently on the bathroom door.

I can hear the concern in his voice. I need to trust my instincts more. Dan's one of the good guys. Isn't he?

"Jess, are you OK?"

"Yep, fine," I call, flushing the loo and washing my hands.

He helps pull the trunk out from under the bed. I unlock it and push up the heavy lid. My old life's in here. Mine and Mum's life and now some of Hanna's too. Mementos. I suppose it's what Dr Harrison would call a giant memory box.

I move aside my summer clothes and Hanna's make-up bag and pick up the inlaid wooden box of Mum's ashes. "Dan, meet Mum. Mum, meet Dan."

"Er, hi," says Dan, awkwardly, reaching out to touch the box.

I place it safely back in the trunk and lift out a threadbare, one-eyed teddy with a ripped ear. He smells musty. Even I don't really want to handle him. "And I do have a cuddly toy. See: Mr T."

"AKA Spooky Bear," says Dan. "He looks like he should be in a horror film, sitting in the deserted attic in a slowly rocking chair. What did you do to him?"

"A minor washing-machine injury, nothing sinister. Though I could never really look him in the face after that."

"After you'd disfigured him permanently."

"I did warn you I'm not a Hello Kitty type of person. Here's the rest of my childhood." I pass him an envelope secured with an elastic band. "There's not much. Mum took a picture of me on my birthday every year and put it in a frame. Until I became a teenager and objected. And she was running out of space. By then *I* didn't need any photos because of my memory – but she liked to have them. She always made a fuss on my birthday."

He takes out the photos and inspects each one carefully. "You were sweet," he says. "A strange choice of hairstyle every now and then. But look how cute you were."

The words 'What the heck happened to you?' hang in the air, waiting for one of us to say them.

"This must be your mum. You look like her."

He shows me a shot of my sixth birthday. Me and Mum smiling into the lens, with her reaching forwards slightly as she wondered if she'd set the self-timer on the camera properly. Mum had made me a Wild West fort cake. Baking wasn't her thing and she'd sworn her way through plastering the kitchen with butter icing and flour. I thought it was amazing at the time and wanted to play with it more than eat it. I can see now it was simply a square cake covered with upright chocolate fingers, a couple of plastic cowboys and six blue candles.

Then the memories come of later birthdays; live-action memories of Mum swooping out of their containment and into my head. I can smell her perfume, remember the sensation of her hand in mine, the swing of her pearl pendant, feel her brushing my hair stroke after stroke as she tried to tame it, hear her laughter as she failed. She's singing 'Happy Birthday', every year, all of those teenage birthdays together in a colossal choir of Mums. It's overwhelming. I sink back and lean against the bed, closing my eyes.

This is why I don't open the trunk. It triggers too much.

Dan sits beside me, our shoulders and hips touching. "I can't imagine losing your mum. I've lost people too. But a parent... What happened?"

"She was hit by a car."

"Jesus, that's terrible." He puts his arm round me. I can feel the weight of his arm on my shoulders and lean into him.

"I see it in my head every day."

"I bet."

"Not like you would. I'm not just *seeing* the images

again," I say. "I'm replaying them, reliving them – the sights, the sounds. I *feel* them again. I remember everything that happens to me, not just what I read." I hesitate to say it out loud. "My memory isn't just photographic or eidetic. I remember everything."

There, I've said it and the sky didn't fall in. Trust him.

"Everything?"

"It kicked in when I was eleven," I say. "No one knows why then exactly. It may be connected with puberty somehow. But after that, yes; pretty much everything."

"So if you did something bad, something you were ashamed of, you'd never shake it off? And if someone does something bad to you?"

"Then I'd never forget it," I say. He looks worried so I smile, nudge him with my elbow and add: "So watch it."

"It makes a guy think," he says. "You know if we ever … you'd always remember my … technique." He's blushing. Sweet. I tell him about my weird memory and he's basically thinking about sex.

"Yep. For ever and ever."

Dan lets out a long whistle.

"Is that really your main question? I'm going to set Mr T on you."

131

"No, not Spooky Bear!" He tickles me until I promise to lock Mr T back in the trunk. He keeps asking me questions about my memory and I have to spell out *hyperthymesia* for him.

In the end, I pass him Coleman's book, *Principles of Memory*. "Read this if you want to understand it better."

Then I take a deep breath and a leap of faith and I tell him: "The unnamed research subject in chapters three to ten. That's me."

19

Try the following exercise using the Ancient Roman technique, placing what you want to remember in the familiar rooms or places: You're in a beautiful house in Kensington. Everything is white. The staircase is wide and grand with a polished wooden handrail...

Work Your Memory

I jolt awake. I heard something outside, maybe a bottle kicked across the cobbles. I give up on trying to get back to sleep and get dressed in leggings and a top. I'll go for a swim. I pull on Hanna's jumper and grab my suit and towel from the radiator.

I enjoy having the place to myself at this time of night. I walk across the courtyard and sit for a moment by the shrine, watching the few remaining candles flickering in the breeze.

But I've a creeping feeling that I'm not alone. I see movement from the corner of my eye. Dr Harrison steps from the shadows. "Ah, Jess," he says. "I thought for a minute…" He trails off. He's unsteady on his feet and looks terrible. "Christ," he says, rubbing at his eyes with the backs of his hands. His foot clips one of the votive candles and the glass holder skims across the cobbles, echoing in the silent courtyard. I take his arm before he falls over. He reeks of booze and stale cigarettes. I'd better move him back to Mandela Lodge, before someone else hears him and I have to explain why I'm wandering around college at night.

The lights are on in his office and there are papers all over the place, and a blanket and pillow on the sofa.

"Are you sleeping here?" I say, realizing I don't even know where he lives. He and his wife must live in one of the staff houses in the grounds, or rent a place nearby.

"Too late to drive," he says, looking guiltily at the half-empty whisky bottle on his desk.

Too pissed to drive, more like.

"He popped round for a chat and the time just flew," he says. He stretches out his arm in a large gesture, knocking over a lamp. "It just flew away."

I right the lamp and see several files strewn across the desk. Student files. Is my file on there? So much for Dr Harrison's promise of confidentiality. I decide to linger and put the kettle on to make him a strong black coffee.

"He was *so* interested in my work," slurs Harrison.

"Who was? Who do you mean?"

"So nice for someone to take an interest in little old me stuck out here in the *annex*," he continues. "Not the *main* building, no, no, no. My wife calls – called – it the granny annex." He falls back into his armchair. "Whoops-a-daisy."

I pick up the papers and make it look as though I'm tidying them away. Dr Harrison's eyes are closing and his head's nodding on to his chest. A little dribble escapes down his chin. He really is a mess. I take advantage. Why not, I'm helping him out and deserve a little payment. I take my chance and look at the names on the files. The first one I recognize is Keira's. Looks like she fixates on death and cries a lot. Big surprise. Not.

The next one I pick up is mine and I glance at Dr Harrison, now snoring, before scanning the contents. There are details of our last sessions and he's written 'holding back' in pencil at the top and given me a rating out of ten. Only a three. God knows what his marks relate to. Interesting anecdotes? Shortness of skirt? I flick quickly through the other files. Someone's recovering from a drug problem in my block – it's always the quiet ones you wouldn't suspect. The others are just the run-of-the-mill homesickness of the year below and a smattering of self-harm, depression and eating disorders. Your average teenage population.

I shove all the papers in the filing cabinet and slam the drawer shut. Dr Harrison stirs.

"We don't want Principal Barker to see this mess, do we?" I say loudly, shaking him. *Or the state you're in.*

"Barking Barker. Woof, woof, woof. Grrr." Dr Harrison dissolves into giggles that shortly turn into gulping sobs. I've dealt with Hanna in this state before, making sure she didn't walk around with her skirt up by her ears, or choke on her own vomit. But I've never had to cope with a weeping man having a midlife crisis.

I give him the coffee, fastening his hand round the handle in case he tips it over himself. I can't believe he's this drunk on a couple of glasses of whisky. With his other hand he reaches out and touches my hair. Inappropriate. I frown at him and step back.

"My wife, you see, she said that I should…" He stares down at his coffee like he's only just noticed it's there.

"What?"

"I thought you were *her*, you see. But the hair's not quite right. I'm not a bad person, Jess."

"No, I know that." *And thanks for thinking I was your frumpy wife.* Her photo's been knocked to the floor so I put it back on his desk. I know exactly where it goes.

"I didn't imagine how it would turn out," he says. "You believe me, don't you?"

He's rambling incoherently. I pass him the tissues for emotional emergencies. He works his way through the box while I wash the glasses and cups and tidy up. By the time I've finished, the room looks back to normal, save for the dozing drunk in the armchair. I put the blanket over him and prop the pillow round the back of his head.

"You owe me. Big time," I say loudly, but he's too far gone to hear. He grunts and shifts in the chair.

I draw the curtains and turn off the lights, pulling the door closed behind me, making sure it clicks shut. It's two o'clock in the morning but my evening wasn't entirely wasted. I learned a few things and, as an extra bonus, Harrison owes me now.

20

*Traumatic memories trigger an emotional, sensory
feeling in the amygdala part of the brain. Disconnecting
the retrieval of the memory from the triggering of those
repeated feelings of fear and anguish would reduce the
trauma on recollection, if not remove it altogether.*

Principles of Memory – *Professor A.E. Coleman*

I don't see Dan until lunch. I ducked out of breakfast
and we have different lessons in the morning. I'm
worried that I shared too much about my memory.
I haven't told anyone all that before. He now knows
I'm not only someone who can remember the useful
stuff to win a competition or do well in exams, I can
remember everything he ever says or does with me.
If we argue, I'll remember it forever. I can hold it
against him forever.

As I'm clearing off my tray, shovelling uneaten chilli
into the food bin, he comes up to me. "Not hungry?"

"No, I…"

"Have you been avoiding me today? That seems to happen a lot with you," he says. "Always hiding. Come on."

He leads me out into the gardens, away from the whispering and the gossipy looks of Keira and Maya. There's a nervous flutter in my stomach I can't swallow away. We stop at the bench on the edge of the rose garden. It's damp from the morning drizzle so Dan puts down his sweatshirt for us to sit on and hands back *Principles of Memory*.

"I stayed up late and got up early to read it," he says. "It's a page-turner when you know what it's really about. *Who* it's really about."

"It doesn't even cover the half of it. And?" I'm trying to read his body language. Does he think I'm a freak?

"I can't imagine remembering *everything* that happens. I'm still trying to get my head round it." He reaches out and takes my hands in his and looks me in the eyes. "Thanks for telling me. It was brave. I'm guessing no one else here knows how amazing you are?"

"No, but it's not amazing," I say. "Someone once said it's a superpower but it's really not. I can't change anything with it."

"So you won't be dressing up in Spandex and fighting the powers of evil?"

"Sorry to disappoint you. It's more of a … liability. I can be … difficult," I say.

He laughs. "I've already noticed. But you don't get rid of me that easily."

We kiss for a long time, until my bottom lip is comfortably numb.

"We can make lots of nice memories too, you know," says Dan, putting his arm round my shoulders. "Can't the good ones cancel out the bad?"

"It doesn't seem to work like that," I say, wishing that it did.

He flicks through *Principles of Memory*. "Bizarre that you were involved in all this."

"Coleman called it the Programme," I say. "It went way beyond what she talks about in there. I thought she was helping me, but, well, she wasn't. All the never-ending replaying images of the accident again and again – the red Range Rover which hit Mum, the CPR – I'd had enough.

"Finding an email in Coleman's files from Mum saying she wanted to pull me out of the Programme, was the push I needed to finally leave. Mum had shown me a prospectus for Dartmeet once, so I came here myself in the spring term. I got away from all that, from being the memory star turn."

I lean back into his shoulder, relieved to have finally told someone the truth. Or part of the truth. He doesn't know they're looking for me, that it's not all in the past. Could they have realized about the money I took? Is that what they're after?

Dan taps at the author photograph of Coleman. "She looks so … normal. What about the rest of them?"

"The nice ones didn't stick around. I never knew exactly what Coleman was up to, how all these different aspects slotted together. I still don't. Her book doesn't fill in those gaps. She kept us in the dark, just familiar with our own areas."

"So there were others on the Programme?"

"At first. The linguists, the super-recognizers…"

"Say what?"

"I never forget a face. But it's not that special – about one per cent of people can do it. There's a whole unit of super-recognizers with the Met Police in London. They can merge with a crowd, looking for known troublemakers, spotting targets that fixed cameras can't reach."

I cringe as I remember the stupid crush I had on one – an Irish guy called Callum. Coleman was comparing the fusiform gyrus part of his brain to my hippocampus in EEG scans. That was the kind of thing that got her excited.

"But she moved me and my hyperthymesia away from all that to a more exclusive part of the Programme," I say. "Basically just me. I don't want to go back to it, ever. She was working towards a big breakthrough but, honestly, I didn't care once Mum died. At one stage, I tried 'overloading'. I figured that my memory must have a limit; that there'd be a tipping point, when new information received plus information stored exceeds capacity. While Coleman thought I was sleeping or watching TV, I was reading, overloading. Everything in her study, everything on her laptops: even boring reports, financial information, every document I could find. That's when I found Mum's email."

I sigh and pick at flaky paint on the bench. "But all that information didn't overload me in the way I thought it would. It didn't make the painful memories go away. It became a mountain of facts and figures swishing around my head."

"But don't you see?" says Dan. "That's where you should start to work out what she was up to. It's all in there." He touches the front of my head. "The frontal cortex or thalamus or whatever you call it. You're a walking encyclopaedia on what was really going on with the Programme. You've *seen* all the information with that amazing memory of yours but you haven't processed it yet."

"Do you think I could churn them out and make sense of it now?" I ask, my brain whirring.

"Why not? You're a repository of her secrets. She shouldn't be allowed to screw anyone else over. I'll meet you in the library after running club. Jeez. And you said you didn't have a superpower to fight the forces of evil!"

He may be right. All those documents Coleman doesn't know I've seen are in my mind-library waiting to be understood. I just need to retrieve them.

21

Certain drug combinations produce pathological disturbance.

Principles of Memory – *Professor A.E. Coleman*

I'm not used to going out with someone. Even the word 'dating' makes me think of forty-five-year-olds looking for a perfect match on Snog.com. But this evening feels strangely intimate, as if I should light candles and stream jazz and wear my best underwear. More so than if we were going to sleep together. I bet Dan's never had a 'date' like this before. At least I'm quirkier than the other girls he's been out with, whose bedrooms he seems to know so well.

We meet in the smallest study room at the library. The librarian stuck up a sign saying 'Keep calm and carry on studying' that someone changed from 'studying' to 'snogging'. You can only fit two people in there and if you wedge a chair against the door you buy yourself some privacy.

"This is cute," says Dan. "I haven't been in here before."

I'm glad. I'd wondered if Keira had featured it, and all its charms, on her orientation tour.

He smells good. I'm getting wafts of shower gel and shampoo.

"How was your run?" I ask.

"Muddy. You'd have hated it. But I'm getting to find my way around the moor."

There's a slightly awkward silence. Stripping naked in front of him would be less embarrassing than this. "This is strange," I say. "Reading my brain out to someone."

"Chillax. This is my first time too." He grins and nudges my arm playfully. "...Of brain intimacy. Is that even a thing?"

I smile back and relax slightly. "It is now."

"It'd be easier if I were Mr Spock from *Star Trek* and could do a Vulcan mind-meld with my fingertips but instead we'll have to use the old-fashioned method of you telling me what you see in your head."

He sits down and gets out a pen and paper. "Strictly confidential. What happens in Memory Club, stays in Memory Club."

I exhale. I've already thought of where I want to begin. I pull Coleman's book *Principles of Memory* out of his bag and hand it back to him. "Page 143, halfway down." Dan finds the page and starts reading, though I finish the sentence with him from memory: "*And certain drug combinations produce pathological disturbance, though they can alter perception of events.*"

"I want to find out exactly which drug combinations she might have been giving me." I don't dwell on the 'pathological disturbance' side effect mentioned. I don't want him to think I'm a complete fruit loop. Saying it out loud I realize how dumb I was to take it all on trust – 'vitamin' pills, injections, drips. Mum had signed consent to everything; we were receiving considerable payments for 'expenses'. But we trusted Coleman.

"Do you remember any mentions of 'mg' or 'ml' or chemical names or symbols?" he asks, pen poised.

I start walking through the mind-library in my head, thinking where I should try. "There were strange lists in the black notebooks in her study cabinet," I say. "She kept it locked but I'd seen her type in the code."

"Let's start there," says Dan. "They're bound to be important if she's locking them away at home."

I go back to my mind-library, make my way to an oak-panelled room, select the shelf for November last year, take down the book labelled 15th November and open it up. All in my head. Then I play the scene as a movie and give Dan the director's commentary.

"That day, she had to work late. A meeting. As I said, I wanted to fill up my memory. To block out the accident and Mum. I worked through the study bookshelves then I tackled the cabinet. The top shelf was full of black hardback notebooks marked with dates on the covers. I thought they might be diaries but they weren't that interesting. Just lists."

Dan clicks on his pen. "Fire away. But not too fast."

I open one up in my head and read aloud the first page: "CV MG 1st October AB 5 ml, 4th October AB 10 ml, ACh 115%…"

I carry on through the book until Dan begs for a break because his wrist's aching. My head's throbbing. I sit back and massage my temples. I'm drained.

"Wow, you're amazing," says Dan. "I'm struggling to keep up. Reading all this would send me bananas."

"What if it has sent me bananas?" I say, lying my head on the desk.

"Maybe take a break," says Dan. "Do something physical instead." He strokes my hair gently and tucks a stray wisp behind my ear. I'm wondering what he means by 'something physical'.

"I'll stay here while you take a walk down to the drinks machine in the Common Room," he says. "I'll research what we found out so far. Bring me a hot chocolate."

I'm disappointed. Maybe seeing me like this is putting me into the friend zone.

I go slowly back through the library and out into the courtyard. I take welcome breaths of fresh air and wait for it to work its magic on my headache. I walk to the terrace and look out over the darkness of Dartmoor. The moon's bright tonight and a rabbit hurtles across the lawn. But I have a strange sensation, like I'm not alone, and turn around quickly. Maybe Dan came down after all. But no one's there. "Hello?" I say to the empty terrace. Footsteps crunch on the gravel. "Quit freaking me out, Dan!" But there's no answer.

I get a grip. I'm letting myself be scared by rabbits or badgers, as Maya or Keira would be. I walk quickly to the Common Room and the relief of a busy room. Here it's all noise and bustle, pool, table tennis and loud music. I say hello to Felix and Makoto and feed coins into the vending machine to get my drinks. A dose of normality's just what I need to stop me hearing things.

*

Dan's looking pleased with himself when I get back to the library. "Prepare to be amazed by me for a change, memory girl," he says. "Are you ready for a biology slash chemistry lesson with a dose of pharmacology?"

"My favourite subjects." He thinks I'm joking.

"Some of the words that kept cropping up are definitely pharmaceutical drugs. AB stands for sodium amobarbital."

"That was used by the US army to patch up soldiers with shell shock and ship them back to active service," I say. "They thought it would block out the bad stuff."

"You *are* better than Wikipedia. Except the soldiers were too drugged up to be much use. It can be used to mess about with sleep patterns too."

"They did that to me," I say. "To see what would happen to the laying down, or encoding, of memories."

Dan taps at the laptop. "It's also been used to anaesthetize portions of the brain to see which parts are responsible for recall."

"I've seen sodium amobarbital written somewhere else, not just in the notebooks," I say. "I need to process where."

"Maybe because it's still prescribed for anxiety in some countries," Dan says. He checks his notes. "You listed another drug a lot too. Propranolol: often used to treat PTSD. It disconnects any anxious reaction from the memory."

"That's what you want to achieve with post-traumatic stress sufferers," I say. "Dampen those emotions. Coleman talks about that in her book."

"L-DOPA – that's synthesized dopamine – and ACh is Acetylcholine," continues Dan. "Both of these act as neurotransmitters in the brain, chemical messengers sending signals between cells."

"Manipulating levels of those is used in the treatment of brain disorders," I say. "I've read journal articles on it."

We press on through the list. A cocktail of drugs all acting on my brain in unknown ways to see what they can do to memory. Page 143 again: *Certain drug combinations produce pathological disturbance.* I don't dare tell Dan how much I think my personality may have been affected. A flash of guilt about how I treated Hanna washes over me. The mean things I said to her when I knew she was struggling. The things I didn't say.

"How do we prove it?" says Dan, leaning back on

his chair with his hands behind his head. "Even if we had the actual books, even if you could match the doses listed in the book with your reconstructions of every day you were there, remembering injections or 'supplements' you took, is that enough? She doesn't actually cite your name anywhere in that list you gave me. Unless … MG crops up at the beginning of all the books you read out. I assumed it meant milligrams for dosage but maybe she has the same pet name for you as I do."

"Memory Girl? But that still doesn't prove anything," I say. "And what does CV mean? We've nothing to show anyone. It's literally all in my head. What sort of evidence is that?"

He's silent. We've done so much and got nowhere.

I crush the empty drinks cups in frustration. "Do you think these chemicals are still washing around my system, having an effect on me? Could I show that?"

"The college has the right to drug test our urine, though they're probably thinking more about grass than an obscure neurotransmitter. Who would do that testing here? They'd know what the test could pick up."

"Dr Harrison," I say, thinking I just can't get away from the man.

22

Continue the room-system technique. You're in a beautiful house in Kensington. Everything is white. The staircase is wide and grand with a polished wooden handrail. The hall has a tiled floor and a hat stand…

Work Your Memory

How to broach the subject with Dr Harrison? He's sitting at one of the long refectory tables by the window. I take my tray and ham salad and sit next to him. He seems touchingly pleased and surprised I've chosen to share his company. I actually feel sorry for him. There's a tomato-sauce stain on his crumpled shirt, a button missing from his cuff and he needs a decent shave and haircut. It won't be long before the Principal puts two and two together and realizes he's sleeping at Mandela Lodge.

"Ah, Jess. I'm going to walk the hike route tomorrow

to make sure it all works. I'm placing stamps and a notebook in a tin at each checkpoint, like Dartmoor letterboxing. You sign the book and stamp your card at each point. Then I'll check the books when everyone makes it back to school; geocaching without the technology." He beams at me. What a saddo.

I tap my teacup. "Peppermint. Caffeine-free today," I say. "To help with sleep, as you suggested."

He looks pleased to have been useful.

"Talking of caffeine and, er, other drugs," I say and cringe inwardly. He looks up, confused, but I plough on with my weak link. "I was wondering how long certain things stay in your body? Drugs – prescription drugs, I mean, not cocaine or anything." I laugh nervously. Dr Harrison stares at me, his fork suspended in mid-air with a piece of spaghetti slowly unravelling. I probably make things worse by adding quickly: "And I'm asking not for me, I'm asking for *a friend*."

He places his cutlery back down on his plate and wipes his mouth with a napkin. He looks pale. "Like what? Painkillers?"

"No, more something like, ooh I don't know, dopamine, amobarbital or propranolol?" I say, pretending those names are on everybody's lips.

He says nothing.

"Maybe anxiety medication," I add, in case he doesn't know what they are. I was stupid to give such a long list because now I definitely seem to know a lot about it, suspiciously so.

He takes a sip of water. He's looking clammy and loosens his tie. Maybe he's been drinking already.

"So would it still be in your bloodstream or hair follicles months after taking it?" I persist.

"That would depend," he says quietly. "Probably not."

"Would someone be able to investigate and prove it after time has passed, like months, or would it only be detected at an autopsy? *My friend* would really like to know."

Dr Harrison stands up suddenly and pushes back his chair, knocking his glass over the table. "Sorry, sorry." He dabs at the spillage with his napkin. "I'm, I'm not feeling well. But the answer is no, these drugs are hard to detect, probably impossible after lots of time has passed." He swallows as if he's going to puke right here, right now, and dashes for the door, clutching his stomach.

Keira sits down opposite me. "Wow, do you always have that effect on men?" She smiles so falsely I want to punch her but I just smile back. She tucks into her spaghetti and I let her take three big mouthfuls before I say: "Poor Dr Harrison. Food poisoning. I'd go easy on the Bolognese if I were you. It's gone straight through the doc."

I leave her spitting out the last forkful on to her plate. Not very ladylike.

I head outside, looking for Dan. Felix tells me he's still down on the tennis courts by the paddock. As I get nearer, I can see he's practising his serve, firing ball after ball across the court. I whistle.

"Hey, you. You just missed me thrashing Felix," he calls. He wipes his face with a towel and pulls on his sweatshirt. His shirt rides up as he lifts his arms above his head, and I can't help looking.

"Want to pick up some balls while I cool down?" he says, playfully throwing me one.

"No, not really," I say, throwing it back at him. "The testing wouldn't show anything now according to Harrison, but he wasn't very helpful. He's ill."

"He's looked rough lately," says Dan. "Keira said he got chucked out of his last school."

"Keira's a gossip," I say. I don't add what I know about Dr Harrison. I prefer to keep that information to myself.

"So what's next on the agenda of the Memory

Club?" He puts his racquet back in his tennis bag and pulls out his water bottle, offering me some.

I shake my head. "The accident that killed my mum. There's something not right about it but I don't know what. I replayed it so much in the Programme but it's blurry in my head. Fragmented. Normally I see things so clearly."

"OK. If you agree to go to the beach with me tomorrow. The Memory Club outing."

That sounds like a date. Walking hand in hand along the sand, a sunset, a romantic picnic, lying together on a blanket in the dunes... "Agreed," I say, before I can change my mind.

"So what are we looking at today?" he asks.

"*Now?*"

"Why not? Nice bench, nice view, no one here." Dan pulls a notebook out of his bag, sits down and pats the seat beside him.

I stretch out my legs along the bench, leaning back against his side. I squeeze a tennis ball and toss it from one hand to the other while I think. "I learned from my trawl of documents at Coleman's house that she was a lot richer than she looked. She was getting huge payments into her accounts from overseas banks." I don't mention the cash and the share I took to tide me over.

"Lucky her."

"And tucked within all that she had a police report of the accident. That's what I want to reread."

I close my eyes to concentrate on the relevant folder and pull out the report. I work down to the main paragraph.

"*The vehicle involved was a Range Rover Evoque, registration BA64 TYR. It was travelling at a speed estimated to be 25 mph within the 30 mph speed limit but, given the size and weight of the vehicle, the pedestrian was struck with considerable force.*"

I squeeze my eyes tighter, trying to block out the image of Mum replaying in my head.

"*The Witness Statement from Andrea Coleman, Professor of Neuroscience at Queen Elizabeth II College, University of London, confirmed that the pedestrian stepped without warning into the oncoming traffic, being distracted by looking at her phone. Professor Coleman was judged to be an extremely credible and reliable witness, who went on to give emergency first aid.*

"*On examination, the nearside headlight and vehicle wing were damaged in the collision, the white paintwork being considerably scratched.*

"*Despite the severity of the injuries suffered, there was*

no evidence of careless or reckless driving on the part of the driver, particularly given the pedestrian's negligence in stepping into the road without warning, as witnessed by Professor Coleman. No prosecution recommended by the CPS."

"*White* paintwork?" says Dan. "You said the car was red."

I swing round to face him. "Yes, definitely red. It matched her lipstick in a macabre way. It's always stuck in my head."

"The report must be wrong then," he says. "The police filled out the form wrongly."

But I can feel that there's something I'm missing. I look at the scene in my head, play it in slow motion. "The car was definitely red. And I really don't remember a phone. Mum wasn't on her phone – she was talking to Coleman."

"So why would Coleman lie about the phone to the police? Did she make a mistake?"

I think of the postcards. *Things are Seldom What They Seem.* Someone wants me to find out what happened for sure. "Was the car red or white? Who's right – me or the police accident report?"

Dan drums his fingers on the arm of the bench then gets out his tablet.

"Because if it's not me, if the car really was white, then…"

"Your amazing memory has made a mistake."

My memory doesn't make mistakes.

"We can check with the car licensing authority: the DVLA," says Dan, tapping at his tablet. "I had to do all this stuff when I got Uja."

I watch over his shoulder as he scans through the guidance notes.

"With the registration we can see what make and model it is, how old, petrol or diesel and what colour it is."

"Can we find out the name of the driver – the owner?" I ask. "Because they could tell us what happened."

"Not so easily," says Dan. "To get the registered keeper of the vehicle I have to fill out a complicated form and I'm not sure we're even entitled to the information. But you're right, it's a good idea to try to speak to the driver."

"If she's happy to talk to us."

"It's a start. Now, let's find out the colour."

Dan types in the registration BA64 TYR from the accident report and the make: Range Rover. The details come up instantly and we scan down to vehicle colour.

White.

"White?" I run through my mind-library, down to the single-padlocked room for that day. I rip off the lock. In the centre of the room on a repeat loop is my recollection. Parts are blurred and crackling. It jumps forward, buffers. But the car is red. And again and again. "I don't understand, Dan. We replayed it in the lab incessantly. She studied my brain and the flashbacks." I look out at the gardens and moor beyond to calm myself. "It was a red Range Rover. It matched the lipstick. It matched the blood."

"Could they have changed it in the lab?" asks Dan.

My mind flips to the postcards back in my room. *Things are Seldom What They Seem.* The past is not fixed. The accident is not what I thought it was. *History is What We Choose to Remember.*

23

With an aging population increasingly falling victim to Alzheimer's, research on memory is becoming even more important.

Principles of Memory – *Professor A.E. Coleman*

The landscape gradually changes as we leave Dartmoor behind and head for the sea. We drive through quaint villages with whitewashed houses and pubs, as the lanes become narrower.

"The beach? In this weather?" Maya had said. "It's nearly November." But she didn't want to miss a chance of a brief escape from Dartmeet College, and she and Keira are joined at the hip like annoying twins you can't shake off, so we're all rammed into the Mini with beach mats, towels, a Frisbee, and the tiny boot full of Maya's photographic equipment. I'd thought it was going to be me, Dan and the sunset but now I think he wanted a break from the intensity of having a memory freak for a sort-of girlfriend.

It's freezing and blustery. The sand's rolling across the windswept beach. I pull up my scarf to cover my mouth and nose, glad I took it from the laundry room. It's one of many expensive items belonging to Lena that she can't be bothered to retrieve. We have a half-hearted game of Frisbee. We soon grow tired of chasing the spinning red disc down the beach and stopping it from going in the water.

Maya shrieks as we run in and out of the sea. Our feet are numb in minutes. Dan drags me, laughing, back to the water and a bigger wave splashes up my rolled-up jeans before I can get out of the way. "I've got freezing wet jeans for the rest of the day," I say.

He laughs. "You can always take them off. I don't mind."

"And freeze to death? No thanks."

Keira starts singing, "*Oh! I do like to be beside the seaside,*" at the top of her voice to be heard over the crashing waves. Maya and Dan join in. They dance around me, splashing and yelling.

"You're all terrible singers," I shout, trying to be part of the fun. But all I can think about is the accident playing on a repeat loop. Red or white car? White or red? Did they disrupt my memories? What's the real truth of it all?

Dan scoops Keira up and carries her further into the sea, pretending he's going to chuck her in. "One, two, three." She shrieks with laughter and hangs even tighter round his neck. Maya goes to her rescue, splashing Dan with big kicks of water and the three of them tumble into a heap on the sand.

"Sand angels. Go!" says Maya.

They've regressed to six-year-olds. They giggle, moving their arms up and down on the wet sand, making shapes. They all get to enjoy the present, just as it is. But for me the past hangs like a millstone around my neck and I find it harder some days than others to shrug the weight off. I stand to one side, making a circle in the sand with my toe, driving my hands into the warmth of my pockets.

"I'm going to the car for a blanket," I say. "I'm cold."

Dan cups his hand to his ear. "What?"

I shout it again, over the noise of the waves.

"We'll see you at the top," mouths Dan.

I turn back towards the car park. Dan gets a proper break from the Memory Club. He can always walk away from it and play sand angels. I'm stuck in it forever.

"This way, darling." An elderly man leads his wife down the steep steps. I stop to let them go first.

"Are we going to make a big castle?" she asks. She's as frail as a sparrow, spindly legs and thin arms, dressed in a flowery sundress under a thick winter coat and a woolly hat. A strong gust of wind could blow her over.

"A castle as big as you," he says. "And then we'll have ice creams."

"Is Mummy coming? And Daddy?"

"Er, they're coming later," he says. "You need to build the castle first." He hands her a bucket and she tiptoes excitedly across the sand, twirling the handle.

He meets my eye. "Alzheimer's," he says. "She thinks she's a girl again. But at least she's happy today. Not agitated." And then he's gone, hurrying after the shadow of his wife. I sit on the bottom step, drying my damp feet on a sandy towel, watching them as they make a sandcastle on the cold beach.

I walk slowly back to the car park and get the blanket. I sit by the kiosk in the only sheltered spot, picking idly at the neat stitching on the name tape on the scarf. I think about the woman trapped in her childhood, the confusion she must feel when her parents, long dead and gone, don't show up. The more her disease picks away at her memory, the more *she* vanishes. I don't want to disappear like that. Will that happen to me too when I get old or will my memory always be 'extraordinary'? I've just had a taste of what it's like for your memory to let you down, to make mistakes. Red/ white, white/red. And I don't like it at all. I shiver and pull the blanket tighter across my shoulders.

"Cold?" says Dan, surprising me from behind with freezing hands placed over my eyes. "I'm getting Maya's camera stuff so she can take some wild nature shots. Then we'll head back, now that I know you're not going to go skinny-dipping." He tries to slide his ice-cold hands up the back of my top but I push him off.

"I don't have a death wish," I say. "I thought *you*'d be straight in the sea, coming from Cornwall. Don't you all get surfboards issued by the council at birth?"

"Ha ha. If I had my board, wetsuit and decent surf, I'd have been in, townie. You'll see in the holidays. I'll teach you. Get you out of that pool. That's something where I'm going to have the edge over you, memory girl. You need some of these for starters." Dan flexes his muscles and places my hand on his biceps. It's not a bad place for them to be and I can feel a twinge of a smile. "That's better," he says, kissing my neck and grinding his cold nose into the warm patch under my chin.

"Dan! Are you coming?" Keira's standing there, arms crossed, ready to spoil my fun.

He unfolds and twirls away. He has a lightness about him here. The seaside is his natural habitat. He belongs.

Unlike me.

*

We squabble in the car on the way back about the choice of music. Dan whacks up the poxy heater full blast but my jeans are still damp. Maya and Keira talk about their gap-year plans. Maya wants to visit the national parks in the US and take photographs, Keira wants to teach English in Japan and I... I don't know what I want to do, what I *can* do, so I keep quiet until Maya prods me from the back seat and demands to know.

"The usual," I say, brushing her off. "Chalet girl in the winter, backpack around Asia." I invent a whole parallel universe for myself where Jess can be anything she wants to be. "College in the US. Somewhere sunny with old buildings and a diner. Maybe I'll join the cheerleading team."

"Yeah, right. Hilarious," says Keira. "You know you'd have to cheer people on?"

"I can see you with pompoms and a cute little pleated skirt," says Dan, cracking up.

"I don't know why you're all laughing," I say.

Even my fantasy life doesn't seem to work.

"I need to pee, Dan," says Maya. "Stop in Totnes, will you? My bladder can't take any more."

He parks up near the castle and we pile out of the Mini, agreeing a time to meet for chips. We split off to find loos or run errands. Dan goes in search of a cash machine and I decide I need a proper coffee.

I head down the hill towards the Italian place with bicycles attached to the walls as art. I pause on the pavement outside. A guy sitting in the window is studying me intently. He must be weighing up the haircut and colour change and allowing for the hat and scarf. But I know him, despite the nearly two years that have passed: the goatee and his baseball cap and dark glasses. My brain has instinctively looked at his earlobes, the dimple on his chin, the shape of his eyebrows, the dark curly hair escaping the hat; calculated the distance between his nose and his cheekbones, and drawn conclusions. And while my brain is busy processing, my stomach's been churning with anxiety and circulating bile so that I want to throw up.

I last saw him in London. I poured a can of Coke over him and his precious gadgets in the recreation room. He was annoyed but I can't be held responsible for the phosphoric and citric acid content of a fizzy drink ruining his laptop. And then shortly afterwards I was switched to the more selective part of the Programme and I never saw him again.

It's Callum, the best super-recognizer on the Programme. So just what is he doing here in the middle of nowhere?

24

The brain has evolved to be extremely adept at processing and recognizing facial features, though undoubtedly some people are better than others at facial recognition.

Principles of Memory – *Professor A.E. Coleman*

There's no point pretending I haven't seen him and he hasn't realized who I am, even though I'm tired of my life being a Jason Bourne movie. So I march right in and sit at Callum's table.

"You look ridiculous in that get-up," I say. "It's October in Devon not July in the Bahamas."

"Hello, Freya," he says. "Charming as ever. Loving the new hair."

"Fancy seeing you here," I say. "Is it to beg for my forgiveness in standing me up 719 days ago?"

"Jesus, no one bears a grudge like you can. I explained

at the time but you went postal about it." He moves his coffee away from me and grips on to it. Just in case.

Callum was always excellent at faces but crap at remembering other stuff like what time he was meant to meet me at the cinema, or whether I prefer sweet or salty popcorn (sweet). He loved that his type had a cool name: the super-recognizers. He always said it with a deep American accent, with his hands on his hips and chest thrust forward, like something from a Marvel comic or a film. Like the film he stood me up for. I can still *feel* the pity of the girl on the ticket desk when Callum didn't turn up that night. I've replayed that evening so many times with all its emotional punch, all the more acute because I was a naïve fifteen-year-old with a dumb crush. This is what happens when you *expect* things from people, *fall for* people. They let you down.

"The Programme's not the same since you left," he says. "She had to shut down parts of it."

"And yet here you are, playing the 'Guess Who' game with me, in glasses and a hat."

"You're so patronizing, Freya," he says. "You always did think you were so much better than the rest of us. I'm being paid now. I earn good money, I travel."

"To Devon? Wow! Exciting! Are you in the Met

unit with the other obsessives?"

"I'm way beyond that. There's serious shit happening now." He takes a mouthful of coffee as if he's a big shot. "The things I'm asked to do: you wouldn't believe. It's not looking for shoplifters and football hooligans."

I know he wants to tell me, to show off his usefulness, especially to me, the star pupil he could never match up to.

"I've been using high-tech facial-recognition software to filter images. People like me, *like us*, are helping to develop it," he says. "But lately I've been looking through CCTV and web images for you."

"I'm touched," I say, but inside I'm panicking. My last stupid hope that he just happened to be here on holiday vanishes. He *is* here looking for me. *Finding* me.

I wiped out every photo of me that the Programme had, every piece of paper and back-up file I could locate. I've stayed off social media, been so careful around any cameras.

"They said you'd change your appearance."
They?
"But I knew you instantly." He holds my gaze and puckers up his lips. I feel the heat in my cheeks and am annoyed with myself for letting him get to me, and

for showing him he has. I remember kissing him, of course I do. He was the first boy I'd kissed.

"I had a lucky break this week," he says. "CCTV taken down here a few weeks ago. I thought it might be you, though you've definitely changed. Blossomed." His eyes flick down to my chest. "So I came to have a poke around but I never expected I'd end up meeting you for a coffee. Funny how things turn out, isn't it?"

I force myself to ask the question: "Why are they looking for me?"

He shrugs. "I assume they want you back. To join me and the rest of the gang. A reunion. The good old days."

This is one of the many differences between Callum and me. He's an idiot who doesn't really think about the whys and wherefores. He has slightly more brain cells than facial-recognition software but not many.

Whereas I'm not an idiot and I expect the worst of people. "They weren't good old days for me. You know my mum died? Did it occur to you, Sherlock, that given my change of appearance, name and location, I don't want to be found? That I don't want to be part of the Programme ever again?"

"I was sorry about your mum. That's rough. But I'm

just doing what I'm paid to do. It's not as if you're in any trouble, is it? They just want their star turn back."

"Back? For what?" I push the panic down deep inside. He doesn't answer. He doesn't know.

We're quiet while the waitress clears our table and wipes off the crumbs.

Callum checks his watch. "Listen, the last train back to London leaves soon. I don't suppose you want to come? See what they're offering?"

"What, like a company car and gym membership? No thanks. But I'll walk you there." *Make sure you're on your own.*

We leave the café and take the street leading to the station. It's getting dark. My phone beeps in my pocket. The others will be wondering where I am.

"Do you remember when we used to hang around in that park near the hospital, getting up to all sorts?" says Callum.

"Of course I remember."

"It was never boring hanging out with you, Freya."

"We bonded over the sharing of synapse information. Who else can say that? Remember the cute rubber caps we had to wear?"

"I haven't said anything about the footage yet," he says. "I wanted to be sure."

I believe him. But I don't believe he'll be able to keep this coup to himself without a reason. "Yes. They were fun days," I say. "How about that Halloween party that turned out to be another excuse for researching trauma? Or the time Brett shut me in a cupboard for the afternoon? Or the time he enjoyed strangling me until I passed out, so he could see whether I still remembered it with fear a week later?"

"Some of the stuff they did to you was pretty out there. You showed that Brett guy when you bit his ear, though. That was the talk of the unit."

I swallow hard. I need Callum to be on my side. "At least having you around for a while made it more bearable," I lie. I take his face in my hands and stand on my tiptoes to kiss him. Hard. I taste the bitter coffee from the café and gently moan when he pushes himself against me. I can feel his interest. We're causing a minor disturbance on Totnes High Street. A passer-by tuts at us, which gives me the excuse to call a halt and lead him down an alleyway towards the railway.

"If any of that meant anything to you, Callum," I say, going for the full wide-eyed vulnerable look, "don't tell them you spoke to me. Keep looking through CCTV. Focus on Scotland or somewhere else far away from here." I kiss him again. "Because what we had meant so much to me. That's why I was so upset with you."

"Really? Because you scared the hell out of me at times."

"It's a fine line between love and hate sometimes, especially with people like us, with our talents." I can't believe he's falling for this rubbish. He and I are not in the same league in the talent stakes. He's a one-trick pony. "And then when I'm ready, when I've sorted out my head, I'll come to you. We can have that 'reunion' you talked about."

I know the tiny little brain cogs are whirring in Callum's tiny little brain. He's computing the best course of action. But the brain cogs are competing with his hormones. He tells me his number.

I halt outside the station. I'm not getting caught on CCTV again.

"So I'll concentrate on Glasgow. Mum's the word," he says, placing a finger on his lips. "I'm glad we met up. Of all the coffee shops, in all of Totnes, in all the world, you had to walk into my one, Freya." He's using a pants accent, as though this is all a game, a joke, for him.

"I'm not Freya any longer, I left all that behind."

"Not many people have the chance to reinvent themselves, to walk away from everything they were," he says.

"It's not as cool as it sounds." *And not as easy either.*

"So what are you really waiting for? Why are you hiding out here?"

I walk through my mind-library and rattle the door of the locked room in the basement. "I need thinking time. Something's not right," I say. "An irritating itch that I can't scratch."

"My advice is try not to scratch it. Something tells me you're safer that way," he says. "Look after yourself." He gently ties the scarf around my neck before kissing me, his revolting tongue pushing deep into my mouth.

I shut my eyes tight until he's finished rubbing his hands up and down my body. I want to wipe my mouth on my hand, spit him away, swill mouthwash, but instead I stand there, pretending to be a love-struck bimbo, waving as he slowly disappears from view.

25

Play the game: Jess packed a one-eyed teddy, a pendant, a wooden box, an envelope of old photos and a make-up bag which belonged to Hanna.

Work Your Memory

When we get back to Dartmeet, I go straight up to my room to wash the sand and the smell of fish and chips out of my hair. I want to wash Callum away too but that won't be so easy. And how long can I trust him to keep his mouth shut before he tells them I'm in Devon – somewhere within travelling radius of Totnes? I've bought some more time, that's all. Before I have to leave, again.

They're going to considerable effort to find me, but for what? To persuade me to rejoin a Programme Coleman doesn't even mention in her book?

As soon as I open the door, I know someone has been in here again while I was out. They've tried but they haven't put everything back exactly as they found it. The drawers are partly open and the clothes inside have been roughly searched, the bedding has been lifted and repositioned. I could go on. To my keen eyes, everything has been touched and looked through. But nothing obvious is missing. And there's no new postcard on the board.

It can't be Callum's handiwork so soon. He'd only tracked me to a potential sighting in Totnes, miles away.

I check the trunk. Someone has scratched at the lock, maybe inserted a piece of wire, because it's open. It's Kim's game again. I check quickly through the clothes for the pearl pendant – still safe in its cloth bag. The inlaid box of Mum and the envelope of old photos are tucked at the bottom. My ancient teddy glowers at me with his one glass eye.

Only one item is missing.

*

"What?" says Dan. He's hoovering out the sand from Uja's boot, fretting over his 'vintage' car. "Why would anyone nick that? A skanky old make-up bag. Are you sure?"

"It wasn't mine. It was Hanna's," I say, "and nobody knew I kept it there." *Except you.*

I pause and wait for him to draw the same conclusion and offer some explanation. But he doesn't. "They could have taken my pearl pendant but they didn't."

"That is weird. So what exactly was in the bag?" he asks, still fiddling about with his flipping car.

"First, the Pill prescribed to Hanna by her family doctor in Denmark. Her name was printed on a label on the side," I say. "But here's the weird bit – there was no such label on the *other* medicines in there *and* that's where I've seen the words sodium amobarbital before. She wasn't getting it prescribed by her doctor."

"So she was taking a drug for anxiety," says Dan, stopping what he's doing at last.

"It seems so. She took stuff every day – pills, supposed weight-loss rubbish." I say. *And I should have intervened.* "But why take it from my room?"

"What about a room search by the houseparents?" says Dan. "A random drug search? Have they ever done that before?"

"Once, with a kid last term. I swear to God, you could get high standing next to him with what he was breathing out. Do you think they're going to call me in?"

"Possibly. At least if they do, you know who was in your room. Are you going to report it?" He shakes out the blanket, scattering sand on to the gravel.

"And say what? My stash of illicit drugs has been stolen? I don't think so."

Something stops me from telling Dan this isn't the first time I've had an intruder. I haven't told him about the postcards either. More lies by omission. I'm working out how long I left my room empty before we all met up for the beach. I took my dirty washing to the laundry on the way to the car park. Was that enough time for someone I know here to search my room? Because the nagging voice in my head won't shut up. Even though it can offer me no rational explanation, it keeps telling me that the only person I'd shown Hanna's bag to was Dan.

*

"I think we should do something major for Halloween," says Maya, flopping down next to me on the sofa in the Common Room. She's waiting for me to say something. So I don't.

"I thought we could go to the party at the Fox and Badger in Saddlebridge. Do you think that's OK? Not too soon, after Hanna?" She mouths this last bit as though Hanna's listening in the room somewhere and about to pop out on us, zombie-fashion.

"Didn't you go to a party already?" I say, as though neither of us remember that she had no reservations about going to the 'after-vigil' bash in B-Block. "So I'm sure it's fine."

"Hanna would want us to enjoy ourselves, wouldn't she?" says Maya.

"I suppose so," I say, but I'm thinking that Hanna would have been mightily annoyed that the official period of mourning was drawing to a close so that we could all dress up as vampires and bob for apples.

"We'll need a pass to go out on a school night," says Maya. "I was wondering if you'd ask Barker or Dr Harrison for permission. I mean, they're more likely to say yes to you, with you seeing Dr Harrison and everything."

So Maya knows I see Dr Harrison, which presumably means everyone knows. I'm officially the mad girl who had the meltdown in the library. "He doesn't prescribe under-age drinking."

"We're not all under age," she says, missing the point. "Pleeease, Keira said she'll sort out old costumes from the drama department if I do the make-up, and I've got an amazing surprise too."

Like that's a good thing. Please don't let it be 'Hanna's Halloween' T-shirts. She hands me a form with the names neatly printed: Maya, Keira, Dan, Jess, Makoto, Lena and me.

"Dan's agreed to drive," she says, smiling coyly at me. "So that'll be nice, won't it? If Uja the Mini starts. And Makoto's driving Lena in her flash sports car. I think they want some alone time. Jess, are you listening?"

I say yes but my mind's still thinking about the missing medicines. No one's spoken to me about them yet. Not the houseparents, or Barker, or Dr Harrison. So I can assume it wasn't an official visit. I tell myself there's no reason for anyone I know to take that bag, least of all the three friends I spent the day with. It'll just be that kid in my block with a minor drug habit. Seeing Callum is making me paranoid about everyone, even Dan.

The only consolation in seeing Callum, and the puzzling part too, is that if they really don't know exactly where I am they can't be sending the postcards or poking around my room. Or why would Callum pretend they were still trying to find me? Why have the Missing Person flyers? Just to mess with my head again?

So the postcards are coming from someone else.

Not the Programme.

"How are things going with Dan?" asks Maya, poking me playfully on the arm.

I remember Dan kissing my neck with a pleasant shiver. As he says, it's good to make new, good memories. I should focus on that, starting with a party.

"You know, you shouldn't feel pressured into anything." Maya pauses, no doubt waiting for me to supply an answer to her massive, nosy question. "You're not as tough as you pretend," she says. "And now, with Hanna gone, you can always talk to me."

"Honestly there's nothing much to talk about," I say, though we both know I'm lying and don't want to share. But I feel guilty enough to give her what she wants on the party front. "I'll ask Harrison for permission," I say.

It could be fun, I suppose, and Harrison owes me many favours after I saved his bacon the other night. I haven't been to a proper Halloween party before. There was one once on the Programme with idiots like Callum. We all watched a couple of horror movies and ate popcorn. It was Coleman's big treat but even for that we had to wear electrodes to monitor the effects of the horror films on our nerve activity.

I tell Maya that I have to hand some work in, which

is kind of true, but she insists on walking with me part way to the pigeonholes, still wittering on about Halloween make-up. She skips off to the drama department to get started. I put my maths homework in Mr Humphries' pigeonhole at the porters' lodge and check my own. A flyer about Hanna's Hike, an audition notice for *Othello* and a postcard of Dartmoor ponies. The now-familiar handwriting tells me:

THE ONE WHO REMEMBERS MOST WINS THE GAME

26

Do you remember how things used to be?
Are you missing me, missing me, missing me already?
                    'Missing Me Already' – Silent Fjords

Maya insisted I report to her and Keira's room at five and now I understand why. She's gone all out on the Halloween look as Morticia Addams in a fishtail dress with flowing sleeves, and a long black wig and immaculate make-up.

Keira's picked a stunning costume for herself too. She's dressed as a female vampire in a long dress and cloak apparently from last year's Christmas production of *Great Expectations*. Her hair's up, swept back from her neck where she wears a black choker. Her skin's pale anyway but Maya's added dark eye make-up and outlined her perfect lips. She looks like she's about to do a fashion shoot draped over a coffin.

I wasn't sure I was even going to come until ten minutes ago. I've been brooding on the latest message. But here I am, figuring that all I have to do on Halloween is turn up and be my usual gloomy self. For me they've chosen more 'living dead' than fashion-model look. Keira's fixed me up with a ripped, cobwebby wedding dress which she says was worn by Miss Havisham in *Great Expectations*. Maya's transforming me into a zombie bride, complete with lesions and bruising. I can't help fidgeting as it's taking so long and I'm fed up of her spooky party mix at high volume. The last touch is the veil, complete with bloodstains. When I look in the mirror, I barely recognize myself.

Dan and Makoto arrive. Makoto's dressed as Edward Scissorhands. He's managed to backcomb his hair so it sticks up in all the right places. Lena's still getting ready; she's not renowned for her timekeeping. Her time being way more important than everyone else's. Not.

I can't lie, I'm pleased to see Dan's reaction. "Wow. You look…"

"Drop-dead gorgeous?" says Maya. "I'm taking the credit for the hair and make-up."

He's rocking a hot vampire look in a velvet jacket and ruffled shirt with a cravat. I can finally see the appeal of all that vampire fiction.

"Particularly loving the rotting flesh on your cheek," he says. "Very sexy."

"Your turn now," says Maya, pushing him into the chair. She applies foundation to make him paler, puts some dark shadows under his eyes and draws in a line of blood dripping from the edge of his mouth.

Keira keeps on about how she and Dan make a lovely couple of vampires and takes selfies of the two of them. She's obviously planned from the start to be the ultimate accessory for Dan tonight.

Meanwhile, I'm the zombie bride with no bridegroom.

"Let's take some photos in the cloisters by the chapel," says Maya. "I can use them in my art portfolio. Grab your cloaks, people."

The cloisters at dusk are the perfect place for Maya's shots. She sets up her camera and tests out the flash and different angles while we wait for Lena to make an entrance. I sit with Dan on a stone bench in the pool of light from the sconces, leaning into him so our bodies touch.

"Do you normally wear a wedding dress on your

third date?" he asks. "Some people might find that presumptuous."

"Third date?"

"First there was Ashburton, then the beach."

"The beach was with the rest of your harem," I say. "So that doesn't count."

"Funny. OK, the Memory Club in the private snogging room then, and now this."

"I try to make an effort," I say.

"Good, because so do I." Dan gets a small box from his pocket. "They're from the antique emporium in Totnes. The guy said they were Victorian."

Keira and Maya crowd in to see what I've got. I open up the box and lift the black tissue paper. A set of dangly earrings: dark and Gothic and perfect.

"I thought they'd be ideal for Halloween," says Dan. He's beaming like a kid, waiting to see what I think.

I pick them up and examine them closely. They have matching ovals set in pewter, each containing a picture of a skeleton, their skulls contorted in agony. The glass casing is yellowed and dappled with age. A delicate silver hourglass hangs off the bottom of each one.

"I love them," I say. I mean it.

And Dan smiles in relief.

"They're *memento mori*," says Maya, leaning over me to get a better look. "So cool. The Victorians were big on death and mourning and reminders of mortality. We did it in art. *Memento mori*: Remember that you will die." She waves her hands in front of my face and uses her best spooky voice. "They remind the wearer that death is around the corner, time is passing quickly like the sand in an hourglass."

"How romantic," says Keira.

I ignore her sarcastic tone and put on the earrings, wondering how many people have worn them since they were made. They finish off my outfit beautifully and match Mum's pendant. The black pearl's nestled in my new cleavage, courtesy of a push-up bra and the low-cut dress. "Thank you," I say, kissing Dan on the cheek.

"Steady on," he says quietly. "Isn't this a PDA?"

Keira's watching us, looking even paler. I guess her evening isn't going to go the way she planned it.

"Tart alert," says Maya. Lena totters towards us in a very short and tight witch costume. Her legs go on and on and her bare shoulders and cleavage are dusted with glitter to catch the light. Makoto swallows as she taps him with her broomstick.

"Boo!" Lena looks as if she's going to eat him alive.

"Do you like it? I got it from the Internet."

"Where, SluttyWitches.com?" says Maya.

Lena finds this hilarious. But only Lena could make a cheap witch outfit look quite so Russian porn star. She's had it customized, spelling out 'Lena' in crystals sparkling on the hem. A small mask covers her eyes and nose but leaves her pouty red lips on show. The clientele at the Fox and Badger won't know what's hit them. "I'm going to cast spells, yes, like Harry Potter."

"You have much better legs than Harry Potter," says Keira. "And tits."

"Keira!" says Makoto.

Lena bats at her with her broomstick.

"What? We were all thinking it," says Keira.

"Now everyone's finally here, I want to take photos," says Maya and starts bossing us about into different poses. She's in her element. I relax. You can't actually tell it's me. Even Callum wouldn't know. And I don't think even he inspects exam board art portfolios.

I run in and out of the arches in the cloisters, wafting my veil, and scaring any passing students. I like flaunting my new earrings and bizarrely attractive zombie look to annoy Keira.

"Trick or treat?" says Dan, pulling me behind a pillar and kissing me.

"Was that a trick or a treat? I'm not sure," I tease, kissing him again. I want to store it up, soak up the experiences, build happy memories. Laughter, desire, friendship, fun. Maybe life *can* take a different path for me. I'm not going to let some cheap postcards ruin tonight.

Maya rallies us for a group photo and arranges us like an album cover for an indie group of misfits. She takes shot after shot. Flash-click. Flash-click.

"I'd be happy messing about here all evening," says Makoto.

"Nonsense," says Maya. "You need to experience a genuine English pub and a proper party. We're *all* leaving at seven."

The others go back inside to have last trips to the loo or to get their coats and car keys but I stay outside in the darkness and walk towards the gatehouse. It's a typical late autumn evening on Dartmoor with a chill in the air and the beginnings of a swirling mist. This place is made for Halloween. I can even hear footsteps running across the courtyard and the tawny owl adding to the atmosphere.

The staff at the gatehouse are in a good mood with bags of fun-size sweets and foil-wrapped chocolate pumpkins to hand out to any callers. I sign us all out ready to go to the Fox and Badger, promising to be back by eleven, and not to drink any alcohol. As long as we all pretend that's what's going to happen, everything is fine.

I head back through the gate and towards the courtyard to find the others. I can hear distant music – it must be coming from the Common Room. As I near the corner, I see a glow of light. Every candle at Hanna's vigil is lit. There are many more than earlier, flickering in rows. So bright. The music's coming from a portable CD player by the wall. I recognize it as one of the Scandi bands Hanna loved – haunting acoustic music sung in a mix of Swedish and English. It's the "Missing Me Already" track on repeat play. Over and over.

As I step back slowly, trying to put more distance between me and the shrine, I realize the new tea-light holders form a word: *TRICK?*

Fairy lights are strung around a new framed photo of Hanna propped up against the wall. Hanna on stage in the play before I joined. *Great Expectations*. She looks so beautifully fragile, *playing Miss Havisham*. I didn't know. I'm wearing *her* costume, now ragged and smeared with fake blood and cobwebs.

Keira put me in Hanna's costume.

The photo of her creeps me out. The way it's lit. She's trapped in that frame looking out at me. I don't want to look at her but I can't take my eyes away. Keira taps me on the arm and I jump.

"Gosh, Jess," she says. "Who did this?"

I shake my head in silence.

Maya joins us, all staring at the spectacle, made brighter by the darkness all around. She steps through the candles carefully to switch off the music. She slips an arm round my waist. "Ignore it. It's some peabrain's idea of a ghoulish Halloween trick," she says. "We'd better go before Barker thinks we're anything to do with it and says we can't go out. Come on. Don't let it spoil your evening."

"I think it's beautiful," whispers Keira. "It's like Hanna's joining in tonight."

And I shiver in the cold air.

27

Sometimes our past comes back to haunt us.
Principles of Memory – *Professor A.E. Coleman*

We head off in the two cars, once Makoto has managed to remove his cumbersome scissor-hands gloves to drive. Maya and Keira complain as usual about the lack of space in the back of Uja, and Maya's spooky sound-effects machine is getting on my nerves before we even reach the main road. She insists on using it at the end of every sentence. She's in complete hyper-party mode. "Wait until you see my surprise tonight," she says, pressing the scream sound again. It's like seeing the shrine decked out has made her try too hard to have a good time and pretend we didn't see it.

*

The Fox and Badger is plastered with tacky decorations but the carved pumpkins in the windows are pretty good. It's the kind of eighteenth-century pub with inglenook fireplaces and low ceilings that does gloom and candlelight well. We take up position in the snug with our complimentary glass of a noxious green punch with floating jelly eyeballs, and a bowl of Monster Munch.

"There's a horror-movie quiz, a buffet at nine and then the disco," says Maya.

Dan squeezes on to the bench beside me with his soft drink. "Jess is an amazing dancer," he says, trying to keep a straight face.

"Ha ha. Very funny," I say, but I actually do want to dance tonight. Whatever's in this punch is loosening me up and I want to let my hair down, cut loose after what happened at the shrine.

We send Lena, her ID and her generous allowance to the bar to get the first round. She's causing a stir among the usual customers. Sherlock Holmes is hanging off her every word. A bunch of locals have come as the Scooby-Doo gang, and Daphne and Velma are shooting dirty looks at Lena, who's lapping up the attention from Shaggy and Scooby.

"*He's* not made much effort, has he?" says Maya. A muscly guy in jeans and leather jacket wearing a skull mask is talking to the barmaid, showing her his ugly tattoos. She's dressed as a black cat with painted-on whiskers and twirls her tail around from time to time. It feels strange that we're out in the real world away from college; the adult world of pubs and nights out and chatting up strangers. Hanna's never coming along. She's not going to be a part of it; forever stuck at seventeen.

Keira hands round the pens and paper and we get ready for the quiz. "I'm expecting you to be amazing at this," Dan whispers to me. "I'll write your answers down."

Lena and Makoto soon get bored of the questions and slope off for the kind of activity it's hard to get away with back at the Dartmeet Common Room. We come second and win a plastic spider. An amazing photographic memory only works in a movie quiz if you've seen the movie in the first place and then hung around to read the credits.

Dan fetches us more drinks. "Lena's black-magic reputation has spread to the gents' toilets. The Sherlock character was saying to a bloke in a skull mask that even Lena's name is sexy as hell. I told them to back off, she's got a boyfriend."

"She should be careful or she's going to get Velma and Daphne chucking a pumpkin at her by the end of the night," says Maya.

"Lena's used to tougher competition than those two," says Keira. "Her dad's Russian mafia, for sure."

*

The buffet's served on a trestle table near the fire. Hot dogs, burgers and chips, followed by red jelly or spidery cupcakes. It's like a kids' tea party but we're hungry and I need to eat something to soak up the disgusting punch swilling around in my stomach. Makoto takes three of everything.

"No toilet paper left in the ladies," says Keira. "Someone's used it all up as a mummy outfit."

"Was Lena in there?" I ask. "She's missing the food." She likes to eat. Lena's one of those annoying people who can eat anything and still be a size eight.

"Nope, but 'Sherlock' was all over a middle-aged woman dressed as the Hound the Baskervilles. Gross."

"Where is she, then? It can't take this long to put on more mascara." I have an uneasy feeling. I look round the pub. Definitely not here. The old guys who were drinking pints seated at the bar have gone and there's no sign of Scooby and co.

I leave the others to their greasy burgers. "Back in a minute," I say. "Leave some processed fat and E numbers for me."

I go outside to the beer garden and smoking shelter where the Scooby gang is huddled under the outside heater making roll-ups. "Have you seen my friend dressed as a witch?" I ask. "You were talking to her earlier."

"Perhaps she's flown off on her broomstick," says Velma, who's sitting on Shaggy's knee.

Daphne laughs and takes a drag on her cigarette. "When you find her, tell her from me that she can clear off back to wherever she's come from."

I'm outnumbered so I resist the temptation to argue with her and walk round to the front of the pub and the car park. Someone is shouting, shouting in Russian.

"Lena? Hey?" I call. Two figures are grappling by the cars near the road. Our cars. And I start to run, tripping over my hem, shouting, "I'm coming!" in Russian.

Lena's screaming obscenities, whacking the other figure with her broomstick. He runs away as I get nearer, jumping into his big four-wheel drive, which has the engine running, and driving off with a screech of wheels as I reach her.

She leans on her car, breathing heavily.

"Lena? What the hell was that?"

"I'm fine," she says. "I went to the car to get my mascara. Some guy grabs me from behind. He's strong but I know what to do. Papa sent me on anti-kidnap training. I stamped on his foot with my stiletto heel, then elbow in the groin and fist up to the chin. One, two, three." She re-enacts it for me, her eyes blazing. "Then while he's bent double I smacked him on the head with this." She holds out the two halves to show me. "He broke my new broomstick."

I've always dismissed Lena as a selfish, rich airhead but she's much cooler than I thought. In the event of any trouble, I'd want her on my side.

Lena takes off her shoe and inspects her heel for any damage. "I tried to gouge out his eye too with my false nails but he had a mask."

"A skull mask?" I ask.

"Yes, like a skeleton. Should I tell the barman or maybe the police?"

I remember the guy in the jeans and leather jacket who was sitting at the bar earlier. I don't want the police here, questioning us all, taking names and addresses, working out that my Jess Wilson details don't match up. "He's gone now," I say. "You taught him a lesson he won't forget in a hurry."

"I agree," she says. "I think he thought I was someone else – an old girlfriend maybe. And look at me. If I complain no one takes a girl dressed like this seriously."

"That's not true," I say, but it probably is. I don't want skull-mask guy to get away with it, but still less do I want the police involved. Could it be to do with me somehow, with Callum? But why would they target Lena?

"I'm not reporting it," says Lena, to my relief. "If Barker gets to know, she'll tell my family, and they'll freak." She laughs. "He looked up and saw a scary Russian zombie bride coming to my rescue. He ran away like a coward. Lowlife scumbag. It's nothing."

She readjusts her mask and dress, and arranges her boobs for maximum impact. "Don't tell the others – I don't want to ruin everything. Makoto's a sweet old-fashioned guy and he'll be upset he didn't save me himself. But we have girl power." She high-fives me. She leans on my shoulder to refasten her impossibly high-heeled shoe, which I now know is a useful defensive weapon, and takes my arm as she totters back towards the pub. "I didn't even put my mascara on after all that."

I squeeze her arm. "Lena, you are my new feminist icon with or without it."

*

The others are dancing already. Maya's rooted to the spot in her fishtail dress but managing to sway in time to the music while Keira's wasted no time in taking over the middle of the floor with her full vamp act. Makoto's face lights up when he sees Lena and she leads him to the dance floor.

Dan grabs my hand and twirls me around. "You missed the "Time Warp". Where've you been?"

"Nowhere," I say. "Just getting Lena."

"I thought you'd forgotten me," he teases, moving in closer to be heard over the music.

"You know I'd never do that."

Lena blows me a kiss. "Let's party."

28

Because I'm not gonna let you forget
I know how things used to be
Are you missing me, missing me, missing me already?
                    'Missing Me Already' – Silent Fjords

"Shush," says Maya loudly. "Are you ready for my secret surprise?" She's had way too much vodka to speak quietly. She stumbles on the cobbles and Keira takes her arm. "The pavement's gone all wibbly wobbly," she says. "It's this way, come on." She presses the sound-effects machine: 'Duh duh duh duh duuuuuh' followed by a wolf howl.

She opens the door to A-Block and shoos us all up the stairs. The third floor.

I've got a sick feeling in the pit of my stomach that we're heading for room thirty-one.

The room I shared with Hanna.

Maya opens the door and switches on the lights. It looks like an ordinary room waiting for its occupants. Two beds, two desks and chairs, a shared bookcase and two wardrobes. Two little bedside lockers next to each other like twins. No belongings. Bare duvets rolled up on a bare mattress with two plain pillows.

The room is symmetrical – you could slice it down the middle between the lockers. But there are differences: sticky marks on the walls where Hanna used to have posters of her favourite bands; dents on her desk where she dropped her hairdryer; scratches on her bedside locker where she kept her many pills and potions.

There's a shiny new lock on both windows, so they can't be opened more than a couple of inches. So that no one can fling the window wide open, sit on the sill and talk about flying, and then crash three floors down.

I lean on the doorframe. I can remember the smell of her – the verbena shower gel, the deodorant, the liquorice sweets her parents sent her from home. I can hear her breathing at night, throwing up and running the taps to hide it, speaking in Danish on the phone to her family. A thousand memories crowd in, playing rapidly on top of each other.

Maya pulls out a wooden board from under Hanna's old bed. "Surprise!" she says in a loud whisper.

"What is it? A game?" asks Makoto.

The One Who Remembers Most Wins the Game.

"A Ouija board," says Maya, like she's uncovered a treasure chest from under the bed.

"It's to contact the spirit world and get messages from the other side," says Keira.

"This is the perfect place to do it if we want to talk to Hanna." Maya drags a bedside locker into the centre of the room and places the board on top of it.

"On the perfect night," adds Keira.

"Is this…?" Dan looks at me. "Is this *Hanna*'s room? *Your* old room?"

I nod. I feel sick. I might actually puke.

Maya and Keira kneel on the floor on opposite sides of the board. "This is the pointer or planchette," says Maya. She's holding it up as if she's in the board game café in Exeter explaining how to play Settlers of Catan. "It can point to any of the letters of the alphabet written across the board, or the numbers, or the words 'Yes' or 'No' in the corners."

"Or 'Goodbye' at the bottom," adds Keira. She sets the torch function on her phone and switches off the lights. Makoto takes the pillows from 'my' bed and puts them on the floor for him and Lena.

"Are you mad?" asks Dan, his eyes flashing. "Ouija boards are not to be messed with."

"Chill, Dan," says Lena. "It's a bit of fun – scary fun for Halloween."

"Hanna would have been the first in the queue to play it, wouldn't she, Jess?" says Keira.

I nod. That's true. In fact, she'd have loved this whole evening with the costumes and fog and a seance.

"Play? It's not a game," says Dan. "I'm not staying. Jess?" He opens the door and waits for me.

But something stops me from joining him. I owe it to Hanna somehow to stick around for whatever happens, and not abandon her to Keira and Maya's game. Maybe I need to play it, try to win the game, whatever it is.

"It's my old room," I say, kneeling down next to Maya. "I'm staying."

The five of us rest a finger each on the planchette.

"It's a big mistake," says Dan. He waits at the door for another minute, still expecting me to join him, but I don't, and he leaves. His footsteps fade away down the corridor. Should I have gone with him?

I tell Maya to get started.

"First we need some more of this," she says, handing

round the vodka bottle. "I should have made cocktails, like Hanna used to do."

"We don't need Dan. He didn't know Hanna anyway," says Keira. "And his dad's a vicar. He probably thinks these boards are the work of the devil." The lighting makes her face look so ghostly.

"*And* he's stone-cold sober," says Maya.

Lena giggles. "I'm not, and I'm ready for anything tonight." She winks at Makoto and takes a slug of drink.

"Quiet now," says Keira. We join hands in our circle. The whole experience is far-out crazy. Edward Scissorhands and a witch in an indecently short dress sit opposite me and I'm holding hands with a vamp and Morticia.

"We call upon the departed souls tonight," says Maya, breaking the circle to play a couple of spooky sound effects. 'Whooooooooo! Creeeeeak!'

"For heaven's sake, Maya," says Keira, grabbing the machine off her and throwing it on to the bed. "You're ruining it. Shut up." Keira waits for silence. I stop rustling in my dress, trying to make no sound at all.

"Place your finger back on the planchette," says Keira quietly. "We call on all those souls lost and travelling at this special time of All-Hallowtide. We call on those tormented between life and death who cannot yet pass on to help us find someone in the spirit world.

"We are looking for our dear, dear friend, Hanna Camilla Carlsen. Hanna, are you there?" Keira closes her eyes, lifts her head and breathes in slowly through her nose.

Lena stifles a giggle and then Makoto joins in, his shoulders jigging up and down as he tries not to laugh out loud.

"Shh. Hanna, are you there?" repeats Keira.

I can feel a twitch. The planchette jerks towards 'Yes'.

"Hanna's here," says Keira. "I can feel it." She opens her eyes wide and stares around at each of us in turn.

"Ooooh," says Maya. "Creepy." Her black wig hangs down over the board and she flicks it back as the pointer moves again.

It comes to a halt at the letter 'I'.

I can't tell who, or what, is moving the pointer as it slowly moves on towards new letters, shuffling back before diving off in a new direction: D-I-D.

"IDID," says Makoto. "What does this mean?"

"Not IDID. I DID, two words," says Maya.

"Let it finish," says Keira.

The next letters are N then T.

"I didn't," says Maya. "She's saying 'I didn't'."

"You didn't what, Hanna?" asks Keira in a hushed voice.

There's a pause. A silence. Nothing happens for a long couple of minutes then the pointer moves quickly across the next set of letters, producing a whole word:

W-A-N-T

T-O

"OMG," says Maya. "Quit messing now, whoever's moving this thing about."

I can guess what's coming. I'm holding my breath. I don't want to make a sound. This time the planchette takes its time, sliding so, so slowly between letters.

D-I-E

"Die. I didn't want to die," repeats Maya. "This is horrible."

"Not fun, not funny," says Lena, gripping Makoto tightly.

"I thought she jumped," says Makoto. "From the window."

"Or fell," I say. "We don't know for sure."

"This isn't actually her," says Maya. "Is it?"

"Did something, somebody, *make* you jump?" asks Keira in a whisper.

The torch goes off and the room's in darkness. Maya yelps and grips my hand tightly. Makoto stands up and fumbles his way to the main light switch. "This is one scary English game," he says. "Can we stop now?"

I'm shaking. 'I didn't want to die' is ringing loudly in my head.

29

Memory is dynamic, not a fixed page of history.
Principles of Memory – *Professor A.E. Coleman*

Dan's waiting for me at breakfast. He has a told-you-so expression on his face as he hands me the jam pot.

I give him the satisfaction without the need for a lecture. It's too early and my head's pounding. "You were right: a seance was a dumb thing to do."

"That stuff messes with your head," he says.

"And mine's messed up enough already?"

He raises his eyebrows and smiles wryly. "It's all baloney – even if everyone's adamant that they're not moving the pointer. The whole thing relies on people's insecurities and on wanting to believe."

"Hanna said, I mean, *someone* said, through the Ouija board that she didn't want to die," I say. "I didn't want to die. Spelled out letter by letter."

"Well, obviously *she* didn't say that." Dan looks directly at me, waiting for me to reply.

"No. Obviously," I say quietly. I know he's right, so why am I so unsettled by it all?

"Who do you think was moving it?" he asks.

"I couldn't work out who was deliberately doing it. I tried."

"It may not be deliberate. You can't tell if they're making unconscious movements." He pauses and crunches his toast. "It could even have been *you*."

"Me? Moving the pointer?"

"Your subconscious could be trying to tell you something. About that day. The day Hannie died."

"Hanna. Only her family called her Hannie."

"Sorry, my mistake. And what did it mean, the 'I didn't want to die'?"

"Nobody *wants* to die. Unless…"

"And Hanna? What about her?"

"I-I don't know. I guess I'll never know if she jumped or fell." Hanna liked being the centre of attention. But even she would have drawn the line at being smeared across the pavement for some extra attention, wouldn't she? One minute she was sitting on the windowsill…

"Oh my God, my head this morning." Maya joins us at the table, with a black coffee and no food. "But honestly, wasn't it the best Halloween ever? The best night ever. When the torch went out at the seance, I mean, crap, I actually peed myself a teensy bit. Sorry, Dan."

"The phone ran out of charge, that's all," I say.

"Or did it? Duh, duh, duh," says Maya. "I sure as anything wasn't moving the planchette. And it can't have been Makoto because his English spelling's still terrible. And Lena was too pissed to spell anything, especially upside down. Pass the sugar, will you?"

If Maya's telling the truth about herself, that leaves Keira.

Unless Dan the psychology student could be right – and my subconscious is trying to tell everyone the truth about what happened. That maybe it was *me*. It was *my* fault Hanna was confused and anxious, that she fell, or jumped. Why would she even open up the window that wide? But I can't say that to him or Maya or anyone. Ever. More lies.

My head hurts. I've got image after image of Hanna again. The sound of her soft body hitting the hard ground. The physics of it all. I stand up to go and sway slightly, grabbing at the table.

"You OK?" asks Dan, reaching out to steady me.

"Sure. Hungover. You designated drivers have it easy. I'll see you at Theory of Knowledge." I leave the dining room before I chuck up right there in front of everyone. My phone's buzzing insistently in my bag. Aside from a very small circle, two of whom I've just left having breakfast, no one has this number. It's a non-contract phone I purchased as part of my minor spending spree when I left the Programme. The display's showing 'No Caller ID' so I don't answer straight away. If it's a dodgy call centre trying to flog me something they'll soon get bored and ring off. But it keeps on ringing so finally I accept the call. All I hear is a click at the other end.

*

Mr Desai's twitchy in class today. He watches the door as though he's waiting for someone to arrive.

"Review," he says. "This is how we embed our memories, transferring them from short-term to long-term. I want you to review the mind maps you drew up for a revision topic of your choice, the mnemonics and your memory palaces. Fill in more exercises in your workbook." He pauses and repeats: "Review your memories. Your long-term memories are still unstable, not set in stone. You need to reconsolidate them. Pull them out, review and store again."

"I get it," says Dan. "He wants us to review." Keira giggles in that simpering, extremely annoying way of hers.

"I've been called away to deal with something," says Mr Desai. "I may not make it back before the end of the lesson. It can't be helped." He packs his papers into his briefcase and fastens the old-fashioned catch. His coat's like something from a dodgy melodrama. I'm struck that he's playing at being a teacher from a movie with the bow tie and the briefcase and the strange turn of phrase. He's watched the Harry Potter films and *Dead Poets Society*, visited a fancy-dress shop and assumed a role.

He pauses by the door and taps the side of his head. "Sometimes everything we need is in here. We simply need to retrieve it." His deep brown eyes linger on me longer than is necessary and then he goes.

"Intense," says Dan.

"Excellent," says Maya. "Free period. I can sort out my photos and do some printing." She's uploaded them to her laptop and edited them into black and white or sepia already. "I'm going to put them straight in my portfolio. We all look amazing."

I go through the shots and ask her to print a couple off for me too. She's surprised but pleased. I love the one of Dan leaning on the arch in the cloisters. It captures his gaze as I walk past, my veil flowing out behind me, which I didn't see at the time. I like the way he's looking at me. The intensity of it. The lanterns are lit all along the wall leading up to the chapel door and the whole shot has the look of a classy black and white film. I can put it in a frame and give it to him as a thank-you for the earrings, like a proper girlfriend would do. Maybe there's more worth to photos than I thought.

I choose between the other shots as Maya goes to sort out the printer. I scroll through the ones of all of us which she did on the self-timer. In the background, there's another figure in profile standing by the chapel door. Somebody photo-bombed us, like a passing ghost. I enlarge the zoom. The figure's leaning to the side as though he doesn't want to be in the photo, but why else stand there? Why didn't whoever it was offer to take the shot for us? They must have seen all the hassle Maya was having with the tripod. I expand the photo more on screen, blowing up the background as best I can. It's blurry, and the face is turning away and obscured by the pillar. But I recognize the coat with the distinctive cut like a Victorian gentleman's frockcoat from a bygone era. It's Ramesh Desai. Watching us from the shadows.

*

I run back to pick up the postcards from my room and go looking for Desai. My memory's reviewing all his TOK lessons and the times I felt he was speaking directly to me. Not so paranoid now.

He's loading bags into his car, the dark blue BMW way too flashy for a teacher's salary. He starts when he sees me.

"Dashing back to Coleman?" I say. I throw the postcards at him. "Finished scaring me half to death?"

"That was never my intention," he says, bending to pick them up. "And I don't work for Coleman. Quite the opposite."

"So who are you, really? When you're not pretending to be a schoolteacher or sending secret messages to schoolgirls? I assume it was you getting Dr Harrison drunk to read his files. I should go straight to Principal Barker."

"No. I'd rather you didn't. And I don't think you will. But I do realize I owe you an explanation." He gestures for me to sit in the car but I step back. "I have a PhD from Harvard in neuroscience and my specialism is memory. I had a brief post in Professor Coleman's department in London."

He sounds like he's introducing himself on a dating show or *University Challenge*.

"You're rather over-qualified for teaching Theory of Knowledge at Dartmeet College," I say.

"I came to Dartmeet to find you: Freya Walsh, the memory wonder child that Coleman liked to keep to herself. A tech-whizz friend of mine helped out. Every time you searched online for certain keywords like *Coleman* or *hyperthymesia*, and accessed certain journals or research papers, you were laying a trail, a cookies profile. And then I got a lead from another ex-researcher, Nadia Hashimi, who said your mother had talked about sending you well away from the Programme to an international college in Devon. The two trails converged and here I am."

He gestures around him, as though he can't quite believe how he's got from Boston to a college car park on Dartmoor.

I'm relieved that he knows Nadia. I trusted her. And if she's confided in him, she must trust him too. "Did you have to be so theatrical about it?"

"First I had to be sure that Jess Wilson was really Freya Walsh," he says. "I had no photo of you, only a description from Nadia. I wasn't even sure you'd still have the amazing memory. Adolescence can mean you grow out of it. But after all you've been through already, I didn't want to trigger further trauma that could irreparably damage your memory." He hands back the postcards.

"So you thought you'd spook me with cryptic messages instead?"

"I hoped you'd be intrigued by them and start reviewing what had happened to you on the Programme. It was safer than me wading straight in. The brain's a delicate organ, more vulnerable than you think. In retrospect, it wasn't my smartest move."

He runs his hand nervously through his hair and looks around. "Someone's been making inquiries about me. I can't stay – not if I might lead Coleman to you. But I'm making arrangements to get you away and I'll be in touch as soon as I can." He puts the last bag in his boot and slams it shut.

"So you're just abandoning me here?"

At least he has the grace to look embarrassed. "I'm on your side."

"I didn't know there were sides."

"There are always sides. You have to make sure you're on the right one. There are people who fear what Coleman's working towards, who want to help you."

"And who the hell are they?"

He doesn't answer but gets in the driver's seat and winds down the window.

My mind is whirring through the black notebooks. "Wait! What do you think 'CV' would stand for in her notes?"

"Cognitive vaccine, of course. The crux of her research." He checks his watch and starts the engine. He pulls slowly away, raising a hand to wave. "Keep reviewing your memories. I'll be in touch as soon as I can. Tell no one, trust no one."

I watch the car pass under the gatehouse and screech away on the gravel drive.

A cognitive vaccine. That's what those lists in the black notebooks were: the doses, the equations, the formulae.

Coleman wants to give people the power to forget. Permanently.

30

Continue the room-system technique. You're in a beautiful house in Kensington... The hall has a tiled floor and a hat stand. You leave by the blue door. You walk along a street of stucco-fronted houses and small front gardens with shiny black railings. You hear a car...

Work Your Memory

I check out Ramesh Desai online as best I can. I read some of his PhD thesis and other articles published in the States. There's no mention of his time in London on the Programme, of course. The dates and his qualifications all match with what he told me, but that doesn't mean that I should fully trust him, does it? And yet if Nadia does...

I go swimming at midnight to calm my thoughts. Up and down, alternating breaststroke and front crawl. Then I float on my back looking at the reflections of the ripples on the roof. I feel like Coleman's closing in on me.

I'm running out of time to find out what I need to know about the past. Is there something she's made *me* forget? Has she dosed me up with her 'cognitive vaccine'?

*

Dan and I have had different lessons today but he's texted me to say he's heard back from the DVLA. I'm in the Common Room, biting my lip and picking at my cuticles. If we can contact the registered owner of the Range Rover, we might find out what actually happened on the day of the accident.

As soon as he comes in, I lead him out on to the decking so no one can hear us.

"I haven't opened it yet. Chill," he says. He checks his smartphone. "The car was registered to a Mr Brett Young of Ainsley Gardens, London SW1. That's B – R – E…"

My heart skips a beat. "I can spell Brett," I say grimly. "And I know who he is and what he looks like. Distinguishing feature: small chunk missing from his right ear."

"Blimey, how well do you know this guy?"

"Well enough to have taken a bite out of his ear."

"Jeez, remind me never to get on the wrong side of you." Dan gently pinches my earlobes. "What do we do now? What does it mean?"

"Brett Young is Coleman's assistant. He's nasty," I say. Just saying his name out loud brings a rush of fear and hate.

"But if the car was registered to him, if *he* was driving?" Dan lowers his voice. "That changes things."

"If her assistant was driving the car, not a random little old lady as I supposedly remember, they lied to me. It means they definitely lied."

And things are not as I remember them.

"All this time I've been thinking it was an accident," I say. "One of those terrible life events that turn your world upside down. An event which Coleman and the Programme ended up using for the ultimate post-traumatic memories test." I take a moment to swallow the lump in my throat and hold back any tears. I can't give in to grief when I need to think straight. "Seeing your mother die," I continue. "That's way worse than anything even that sadistic thug Brett had dreamed up for me before. But I've always thought Mum stepped off the pavement without looking. *I saw it.* There was nothing the driver could do, whoever they were. At least, that's what I remember. Or thought I did. Is any of it true?"

Dan looks at the view across the gardens and breathes

out deeply. "We know the colour of the car and the driver are both wrong in your memory," he says. "So maybe this mantra you have that there was nothing anyone could do is wrong too. Brett and Coleman are the ones who fed you that line."

I'm revisiting the single event in the deepest room in the deepest basement of my mind-library and I'm scanning the scene. But it's blurry, it's unclear. "I'm looking through frosted glass," I say. "Why can't I see it better?"

"You were out of it at times with the shock and whatever pharmaceutical crap they were giving you. You've replayed it so many times, how can you possibly know which version is true?"

"But *my* memory," I splutter, "*my* memory is…"

"Is infallible?" says Dan. "Really?"

We go back inside, realizing we've shown it isn't. It's flawed like everyone else's.

I fold my arms and chew my lip again, trying to process it all while Dan gets us a couple of snacks from the machine. He hands me a chocolate bar and we sit on a clapped-out sofa, side by side. A couple of students in the year below come in to play a noisy game of table tennis. Like nothing has changed in the world.

"When I was seven, I went to the beach with my

cousin," says Dan. "We got Mr Whippy ice creams from the van. I had mine for literally thirty seconds before I tripped and dropped it on the sand. I cried. My cousin gave me his one."

"Sweet of him."

"But what if I see a photo of that day and we're holding ice lollies instead of big ice-cream cones of Mr Whippy. Which version is true? The Mr Whippy ice cream I remember or the Fab ice lollies in the photo?"

"It could be a photo of a completely different day," I say.

"If I make the connection enough between the day out and the photo, or what my dad says about it, I might 'remember' it as the day I dropped my ice lolly and be convinced that's the truth of it."

"*Your* brain unintentionally stores false memories. The invented parts have been woven in by your own imagination or by what others, your dad, your cousin, have told you. There's a famous study where loads of participants were easily convinced that they'd once got lost in a shopping mall as a child when they hadn't at all. Memory is dynamic. But my brain is … extraordinary."

"Is that your only argument?" says Dan. "Why shouldn't your mega-memory be misled like mine?

224

I'm not saying it would have been easy."

"If the full machinery of the Programme had glided into action to change my memories, you mean?"

"Isn't that exactly what they did do, after the accident?" he says. "All while supposedly taking care of you?"

I breathe out slowly. "I think 'CV' in her precious books stands for 'cognitive vaccine'. She was trialling the drug regime to create the winning cocktail."

"A vaccine to change memories?" says Dan.

"Yes, and now the accident itself doesn't seem so accidental if Brett was driving the car."

"A whole new level of twisted."

The table-tennis game is getting rowdier. Dan and I lean in towards each other and I say quietly: "We're saying they *engineered* a traumatic incident so that they could test me on it, try out the cognitive vaccine?"

"Why not?" he says. "It's just a bigger version of what you say this Brett guy was doing to you on a weekly basis."

"A bigger, *deadlier* version. My mum…"

"The ultimate traumatic memory," Dan says. "I mean, what a mad way to be. Amoral, unethical, illegal." He runs his hand up and down my arm.

"So what really happened that day? I don't know any

more." I sink back and close my eyes.

"There's a real version in that amazing head of yours somewhere," he says.

"Maybe," I say.

"We need to think what we do with this."

But I'm thinking about the hypnotherapy practitioner certificate on Dr Harrison's wall and whether I can trust him.

31

From the days of Franz Anton Mesmer in eighteenth-century Vienna to the present-day entertainment of stage magicians, hypnosis has had an uneasy relationship with science. For what is it but a state of suggestibility, wholly unmeasurable? And yet some would swear that it works.

Principles of Memory – *Professor A.E. Coleman*

Dr Harrison is surprised to find me waiting at the door five minutes early for counselling. I'm usually late to make the session as short as possible. But today I have plans to lull him into a false sense of usefulness and then strike with the killer request.

We take our usual positions, mine in the saggy, flowery armchair, his in the leather one. The custard creams are counted out and carefully placed on the small plate on the table, and we each have a mug of tea. His hand shakes slightly. From the strong smell of peppermint breath spray, I'm guessing he's been drinking again. But at least he hasn't dashed from the room clutching his stomach yet.

"So how have you been?" he says. "Any more…?" No doubt he's casting around for the politically correct word.

"Meltdowns?" I offer. "Offensive language in the library?"

"Quite so. We all have times when we can't cope, when the pressure cap blows off." We both know he's talking about himself now but pretend it's still about me.

"Vulnerability is not a weakness," I intone solemnly, like one of his fortune-cookie sayings, and he smiles gratefully at me. "In fact, I was thinking about what you said when I met with you and the Principal, about how a recent tragedy can stir up the past." I reach over and take a tissue to build up the dramatic tension as he leans forward eagerly on the edge of his chair. He removes his pen lid ready to scribble notes in my file. What a privileged position he has here at Dartmeet, hearing the secrets of teenage souls, being trusted to sort them out and make things better when it's obvious his own life is one big mess. He must live for revelations such as this to brighten up the usual fare of humdrum anxieties and depression. To make him feel better about his own miserable life and reassure him that he can exert control over something.

"It's made me think a lot about my mum's death," I say. And in case that's not enough for him to get excited about, I add: "She died in an accident, right in front of me."

"Aha. Why didn't you say before?"

"Because I was at a new school, a fresh start, and I didn't want anyone to feel sorry for me. I'd hate that." *And it's nobody else's business.*

He leans over and rests a sweaty hand on my knee. "People would want to help. *I* want to help."

I tolerate his hand today. I've noticed he does it at least once in his sessions. I'm pretty sure it's not in the Counsellors' Guide to Good Behaviour. Is it what he used to do with Hanna? Does he like girls to be needy and vulnerable?

"And I'd done so well to bottle it up," I say, sniffing. "But I guess, after what happened to Hanna, it's spilling out."

His hand gently squeezes my kneecap. "We've spoken before about the five stages of grief. There really are no easy shortcuts. It's a process you must go through to come out coping on the other side. Bottling things up is not the way to go."

I smile and nod back, as though I now realize he was right all along and what a fool I've been not to have listened to him before. "So will you help me?" I say with a gentle break in my voice. "Because I've not been sleeping well. I've been replaying the accident in my head but something's not right."

He nods eagerly.

"I need to remember exactly what happened," I say, my lip trembling.

"Good idea," he says. "Face it head on."

"So I need you to use hypnosis."

His face drops and he sits back in his chair. "I don't know, Jess. I haven't used hypnosis for a long time." From the way he's reacting, I'm guessing his certificate of competency to practise is out of date but he doesn't want to own up to having a big fat lie on the wall. Next to his other dodgy certificates. But I don't care. I can't do it by myself.

"You said that you'd help me." I've already had to tell the man more than I wanted to about the accident to get this far. "It's haunting me, not being able to remember exactly what happened to her. I need to revisit the day my mum died to move on, to get closure." I use the language of counselling to sell him the idea.

"Sometimes the brain prefers not to remember," he says. "It's a useful defence mechanism. We could be opening up Pandora's box and once it's open we can't put everything back to the way it was. It's a risk." He gets up and walks to the window, looking out across the courtyard. "I don't want to make matters worse for you," he says quietly.

I honestly don't think things can get any worse. But to him I say: "I'll take the risk. It's all on me." He still doesn't turn round. I hoped I wouldn't have to spell it out but here goes: "And you owe me. That night, remember?"

He sighs and sits down, this time behind the desk, at a distance. I've crossed a line he didn't think I'd cross. "Hypnosis is not a precise science. Even if I do as you ask, I can't promise that it'll get the result you're after."

"I know that."

"Patients are suggestible in a hypnotic state," he says. "Many so-called recovered memories are false but the patient vehemently believes them to be true."

"So don't 'suggest' anything to me when I'm hypnotized. Just ask questions. I'll bring Dan so he can take a record and we can be sure of who said what."

"And it's questionable ethically."

"Then it's our little secret. Strictly between us."

I pause. "Like what happened the other night."

His eyes flit to the window and he lowers his voice. "You leave me little option. I suppose if we keep it to ourselves…"

"Yes – definitely. It must all be strictly confidential. You're bound by patient confidentiality, aren't you?"

He rubs his temples with his fingertips and sighs deeply; a resigned sigh. "All right. I'll dig out my old books and refresh my techniques. We'll fix a time when we won't be disturbed. Maybe when everyone else is at the Friendship Supper tomorrow."

"I'll have a migraine and skip it," I say. "See you at six tomorrow."

I'm one step closer to finding out the truth.

32

Sometimes we just need a cue to retrieve a memory;
a Proustian moment of involuntary recall sparked
by a taste or smell from our past.

Principles of Memory – *Professor A.E. Coleman*

"You'll never guess," says Maya, dashing up to us in the lunch queue the next day.

"Why bother if we'll never guess?" says Keira.

"Is it to do with the hike planning?" I ask, hoping it's not and wishing that I'd never been roped in to help with it.

"No, silly!"

"Then I give up." I go back to selecting a topping for a jacket potato, which is usually more interesting than keeping up with Maya's gossip.

"Ramesh Desirable has gone. *Il a disparu*," Maya

says with dramatic flourish.

"We know," I say. "He left our lesson, remember. Something came up."

"No, he's actually gone. For good," says Maya. "I overheard Barker on the phone. I went to top up my printer card in the office and I heard her because her door was open. '…completely left us in the lurch,' she said, 'not answering his phone and appears to have cleared out all his belongings from his room.' Barker was livid. Saying how she couldn't get Ms Mac back at such short notice and how irresponsible he was, etc. etc. Maybe he's been caught with his pants down in the stationery cupboard? Clearing off before it gets out."

"Phoebe Fitzpatrick in Year 12 was always flirting like mad with him – flicking her hair and hanging on his every word," says Keira.

Just like Keira with Dan. It takes one to know one.

"But then I sneezed," says Maya. "You know when your nose is so itchy and you try to stop yourself from sneezing which only makes it worse? And I couldn't help it. So Barker stopped talking and came to the door of her office and asked me what I wanted. I stammered something about the printer card but I don't think she believed me. I would *not* make a good spy."

"Maybe he's gone off with Phoebe," says Keira. "We should check."

I stand there listening to all this gossip and speculation, pretending I'm finding it riveting while knowing his sudden disappearance has everything to do with me.

Keira's theory is blown out of the water when we spot Phoebe Fitzpatrick on her way to play tennis. She's swinging her racquet and laughing. If she's heartbroken, she's hiding it well.

"Unless she's hired a stunt double, she definitely hasn't run off with Mr Desirable." Keira sounds disappointed.

I leave her and Maya working on their next theory.

*

I go back to my room, sit at my desk and close my eyes. Will I get closer to the truth after putting myself through hypnosis with Harrison tonight?

There's something nagging at me from earlier, fighting for my attention amongst the mass of information. Review your memories, Mr Desai said. Everything's in there, you simply need to retrieve it. I've got all the pieces of the puzzle but I can't see the whole picture.

I open up the window and enjoy the blast of cold air like Hanna used to do. The photos of us at Halloween, which Maya printed for me, blow on to the floor. As I prop them up again on my desk, I catch a glimpse of Lena outside and I realize what's been troubling me. I run downstairs and intercept her.

She smiles broadly at me. "Ah, my fellow ninja," she says and kisses me on both cheeks.

"Lena, at the Fox and Badger, why did you say that man in the car park thought you were someone else?" I ask.

"Oh, because of the only thing he said, apart from the swear words after I hit him. As he grabbed me, he said: 'Trick or treat, Freya?'"

I go straight back to my room and pull out Lena's scarf from my chest of drawers. The one I was wearing when I saw Callum, when he fondled me with my eyes tight shut. He's smarter than I thought. He sent someone to find Lena Petrova. Her name tape, which I'd casually picked at on the beach, is gone.

33

I summon up remembrance of things past
'Sonnet 30' – Shakespeare

The lights are dimmed in Mandela Lodge, the curtains drawn. Dr Harrison has seated me in the flowery armchair and pulled up his desk chair to a few inches away. He looks nervous. There are tiny beads of sweat on his upper lip and forehead. His breath smells of garlic and stale cigarettes. I'm focusing on his nose hair to concentrate. Dan sits on the small sofa ready to record everything.

Dr Harrison reviews his notes again and fiddles with his fountain pen. I gave him a summary of the accident, without mentioning my amazing memory or the Programme. His bushy eyebrows briefly shot up into his hairline but they've stabilized now.

"I wish you'd shared what happened to your mother earlier. Dealing with not one but two deaths in close succession is a tall order for anyone. I could have helped."

I doubt that very much. And I don't think his help was much use to Hanna. But I need him to feel indispensable today so I nod. "I just didn't know how to begin with it all," I say, perfecting my vulnerable look.

His hand hovers near my knee again. I cross my legs and look over at Dan, who's fiddling with his phone. Harrison pulls back to adjust his glasses. "People have different tolerances for hypnosis," he says. "If you resist at all or show any scepticism, it won't work."

It'll work. I've had plenty of experience of people delving into my brain. I've sat patiently while the full technological armoury has scanned me. Anyway, there's only one way to go with all this. I need to go through with the hypnosis and review what I actually saw the day of the accident. Callum has obviously told them 'Lena Petrova' is my new name. He knows I did Russian on the Programme. And they managed to track Lena or her car to the Fox and Badger. So even if they know now she was the wrong person, it won't be long until they come to check out Dartmeet College. And this time I won't have the benefit of a full disguise. I'm running out of time to get to the truth.

"Let's begin," says Dr Harrison. "First I want you to tense your muscles. Make fists with your hands, scrunch up your toes. And release. And repeat. As you release, you feel the tension draining from your body. Focus on your breaths and the sound of my voice. Nothing else exists beyond this room. Breathe in for four and out for four. Empty your mind." His voice grows quieter.

It's an impossible task for me to empty my mind, but I can battle to subdue it. In my head I'm running around my mind-library, pushing doors shut, dimming the lights, shutting out the memories. Me aged twelve watching a Christmas movie with Mum; my thirteenth birthday treat of ice skating and a cake decorated as an ice rink; the complete Harry Potter movies trying to burst into my vision…

"We're focusing on the rise and fall of your chest," says Dr Harrison. "One, two, three, four."

My mind's still racing – the university department, Coleman's house in Kensington, Dartmeet. So many memories, so many objects.

"As you listen to the breaths, so you will start to feel more relaxed. Now focus on my finger," he says, holding up a nicotine-stained index finger.

I look up at it, trying not to blink, staring at the lines around the knuckle, the flecks of dirt under his nail.

"As you look at my finger, your eyelids are getting heavier. Your whole body is feeling heavier. It's OK to shut your eyes now. We're descending a ladder and as we count down the rungs you will go further into the trance. One, two…"

My eyes are so heavy they fall shut. I can't open them. I want to drift into sleep. Dr Harrison is counting, but he sounds so far away – like he's in another room. I climb down the ladder, my hands gripping the sides. I can feel the wood beneath my palms.

"Each step down is taking you deeper and deeper."

I'm giving in to it. I can feel myself descending.

"And ten."

I'm in a fog. A muffled fog. A clock's ticking loudly and then it chimes.

"We're going back to the day of the accident: September the twenty-first last year. Picture yourself first thing in the morning. Where are you?"

"I'm in my bedroom at Coleman's house in Kensington. It was easier for me to stay there so I didn't have to travel so much from Mum's."

"Good," he says. "Describe that room."

"Everything is white: the walls, the furniture, the bedlinen. I'm a messy splodge of colour in her clinical home."

"What happens next?"

"The doorbell rings. I hear the clack of Coleman's heels in the hallway going to answer it. Brett's due to drive me to the testing unit at the hospital so I get my bag together."

"And then?" His voice sounds so far away. My chest is tightening. I begin to speak more quickly, the words tumbling out.

"I go down the stairs. The staircase is wide and grand with a polished wooden handrail. The hall has a tiled floor and a hat stand. The door to the study is shut but I can hear voices. Coleman and Mum. I didn't know I was seeing Mum that day. I can't wait to see her. I place my hand on the doorknob but I stop myself bursting in because their voices are raised. They're arguing."

"What about?" asks the distant voice.

"Me? Yes, they're arguing about me. Mum's angry. I hear snatches. She says: 'What have you done? She's changed – different – colder…'

"'Your daughter's crucial to the whole Programme; the linchpin,' says Coleman. She sounds furious. 'Her remarkable memory is at the centre of everything we do and how we test our progress. You can't pull her out.'

"'You may have all these fancy qualifications and everyone who works for you wrapped around your finger but that doesn't work with me,' shouts Mum. 'My daughter is leaving with me today.'

"I draw back from the door as Mum comes out. Her face is flushed. She hugs me and kisses me on the cheek and holds me again. She tells me calmly to get my things. Her red lipstick leaves a sticky trace on my cheek.

"Coleman is saying she'll think about scaling back my involvement, I could move back home sooner than planned. She's asking Mum to go to the department office with her, to pick up her cheque. Mum's hesitating, but Coleman says we have to all go, now, or she won't get the final payment. Coleman says she'll get Brett to drop my things off later. She goes to the study to phone him. Mum powders her nose, applies red lipstick. Her warpaint, that's what she called it."

I try to squeeze my fists but I can't feel my fingers properly. My heart's pounding. Everything is blurry but it's slowly clearing, coming into focus.

"We open the blue door and turn left past the stucco-fronted houses and small front gardens with shiny black railings. Mum's ahead of me; she's talking to Coleman. They're arguing again. They stop on the corner. A white car is moving fast past me. Coleman looks up and her arms move forward. Mum stumbles backwards into the road, into the car. The car was white. But now it's red with Mum's blood. It matches her lipstick.

"Mum didn't stumble for no reason.

"Coleman pushed her."

34

The truth comes out like oil on water.

Yiddish proverb

I want to get out of here. My heart's going to split in my chest.

"Bring her back!" someone shouts.

Who? Who's shouting? They're so far away.

I need to get up a ladder. I must climb up but I'm fumbling. It's not a real ladder, I know that, but it feels like one, swaying under my weight. It's not strong enough to take me back.

A distant, frantic counting: "Ten, nine, keep going, Jess, eight, seven."

It's not real. But Coleman's following me up the

ladder. How can she do that?

It's not real.

Or is it real?

Coleman's hand fastens on my ankle and I fall back a rung. I'm shaking my foot and gripping the wooden sides.

"Six!"

"What's wrong with her? What have you done?"

I don't like the shouting. Who's shouting? Is it Coleman or Mum? I recognize the voice. Who is it? If I could only open my eyes properly. They're so heavy. I'm so heavy, all of me. I could slip back down into the quiet and curl up in a ball. Back down there.

"Jess! Get up the ladder. NOW." Is that…? Is it Dan?

I flick my foot and Coleman falls back. It's not real. It's not real.

"Three, two, one and open your eyes!" Dr Harrison's face is in front of me. I try to see my face reflected in his glasses but the room's spinning. I grip the armchair to steady myself.

"Jesus. You gave us a scare," says Dan, kneeling beside me.

Is *this* real now? Is this room back to real life? "What did I say?" I whisper. My voice sounds strange and husky, like it belongs to someone else.

Dr Harrison wipes his face with his handkerchief. "Thank God," he says. "Never ask me to do that again."

"I thought you were having a fit or something," says Dan. "You went from slumped in the chair to kicking out." He hands me a glass of water and I sip slowly, running my tongue over my dry lips.

Harrison takes my pulse. "That's better. Much better. How do you feel now?" He makes notes like a proper doctor.

"Groggy. Like I've been to an all-night party and drunk neat vodka."

I hold out my hand. It's still shaking gently. "That felt like hours. I must have said a lot." I look at the clock: 6.20 p.m., which can't be right.

"You were in a deep trance for fifteen minutes. That's all," says Dan.

"Which was far too long," says Harrison. He opens up his desk drawer and pours himself a whisky. "For medicinal purposes," he says, more to himself than to us.

My legs feel strong enough to stand now. "I'm OK," I say. "But did it work?"

Dan nods. "Oh yes. I recorded it all." He places his finger on his lips and tilts his head towards Harrison, who's on his second glass of medicine.

"Thank you, Dr Harrison," I say, though I'm not sure he hears me, and we slip away from the room.

*

Dan's played the recording. We sneaked him into my room again and I lay back on the bed in the dark to listen while he held my hand. It's hard to take it in. I'm shaking. I've now finally seen the real memory: Coleman deliberately pushed and killed my mother. Those feelings are back, being numb and broken.

"They must have manipulated your memory on the Programme afterwards to cover it up, used the cognitive vaccine," says Dan. "Brett drives the car, Coleman pushes her. It's insane." He strokes my hair softly. "We should go to someone with this. The police?"

I shrug him off and stand up. "With what? A recovered memory from a grieving, messed-up girl? Harrison said hypnosis is notoriously unreliable. And you haven't met Coleman. She's so plausible. She's a leader in her field. No one would believe me over her." I pace up and down the room trying to see a way forward. Does Desai know all this? Is this what he was pushing me to find?

"She must have had help somewhere along the line, covering this up," says Dan. "Maybe she paid people off, police officers even?"

"She has ways of getting what she wants," I say. "All the time."

"But to do that – pushing a living, breathing person into traffic," says Dan.

"It seems she took a quick decision to do it." Am I making excuses for her? I don't want to believe it was meticulously planned, *deliberate*.

"Or maybe she always planned to do it but brought it forward when your mum kicked off. It's so mad," says Dan.

"Agreed, but it enabled her to show that she can change a traumatic memory. That even a mind like mine can be manipulated with her techniques. It was to get rid of a problem – Mum – *and* to do the ultimate experiment."

"Win-win," says Dan, doing air quotes with his fingers.

"They'd already done all that research on the way memories are laid down and how to improve or disrupt that with reconsolidation therapies. The role of sleep, spatial games, drugs. They'd observed me."

"Observation. You know how it works with

scientific method and experiments – we're taught to use it ourselves." Dan sits at my desk and grabs a clean sheet of paper. "Observation, Hypothesis, Prediction, Experiment, Conclusion."

I lean over his shoulder. "Hypothesis: Can even the girl with the *best* memory in the world, *me*, the perfect photographic and hyperthymestic memory, be made to forget something traumatic?"

"Prediction," says Dan. "If they can do it with you, they can do it with any memory. They can do it with anyone. That's why *you* were so crucial to their research."

And why they're looking for me again? The super-memory girl.

"So they stage the 'accident', followed by weeks of 'treatment' and reconsolidation therapy," I say. "And I was too shocked or drugged up to realize. The experiment in action."

Dan counts off down the paper: "So Observation, Hypothesis, Prediction, Experiment and…"

"Conclusion: it worked," I say. "They can change memories. They can remember it for you."

"It worked *at first*," says Dan. "Their methodology is flawed. There's no control group. There's only one memory girl. You."

"And I've always known something wasn't right," I say. "That memory wasn't stable."

"Your mum suspected they were giving you something which had changed your personality – so there were definite side effects."

"From the cognitive vaccine," I say. "A drug combination to change memories."

"Maybe for it to keep working, it requires ongoing medication," says Dan. "It's not a literal one-off injection. It's a more complex combination of drugs…"

"And procedures."

"You running away from the Programme stopped all that."

"As far as they're concerned, it worked and I still don't know what really happened," I say. Part of me wishes that was still the case. It's disturbing to know that a memory that felt so convincing, which I've grieved and obsessed over, is unreliable. "But I don't want to make matters worse by Harrison turning detective or asking awkward questions."

"He was concentrating on trying to end it once you got agitated," says Dan. "He was freaking out that he'd harmed you. You were speaking so quickly; without the recording and knowing the background, it wouldn't have made much sense."

"Maybe. But I'd feel happier if I got my file off him."

"He shouldn't have been doing hypnosis in the first place," says Dan. "So he's not going to own up, is he? And from what I hear, he's got enough to worry about. His wife's chucked him out and he's sleeping at Mandela Lodge on the couch. He hides the bedding in the cupboard, Keira saw it."

Keira again.

"We'll get his notes somehow," I say.

Dan pulls me on to his lap and wraps his arms around me. "Are you going to be OK? Now that you know what they did to your mum?"

"I don't know yet," I say, my mouth dry.

"And now that you're mortal?"

"Mortal?"

"Turns out you're not infallible, memory girl."

He's right. My super-memory isn't perfect. If memories make us who we are, what happens when those memories turn out to be false? Who am I now?

"At least I know Mum was fighting for me," I say. By leaving the Programme myself, I'd granted her wish. Her *last* wish. I'm unsteady still; the rug has been whipped away from under me. I close my eyes and sink my head on to Dan's shoulder. We're discussing this too rationally, like an actual science experiment in my biology paper on the diploma.

Whatever the truth, the result's the same. Mum's still dead. But they caused it and now I need to fight for the truth for Mum too. Because I know what Coleman was doing and how she used me. And used Mum.

After everything I did for them, I was just another lab rat.

35

Try the following memory exercise: Read each word once. Close the book and write down as many as you can remember:

torch	*drugs*
file	*photos*
bottle	*cigarettes*
secrets	*lies*

Work Your Memory

I've given Dr Harrison a full day to write up any notes on me – before I steal them back. Dan and I lurk in the courtyard waiting for him to leave Mandela Lodge for the lecture room. As expected, he leaves his room ten minutes before the start of the briefing on orienteering and map skills for the Hanna's Hike participants. A box overflowing with maps balances awkwardly on his thigh while he locks the door.

"Won't he notice we're missing?" whispers Dan.

"We'll be so quick, we'll be there before he's handed round the compasses," I say. I do a final check that no one's looking then point at the window which he always leaves slightly ajar for ventilation. It's narrow but possible. Dan makes a stirrup with his hands and I push off him to reach the edge of the window frame while he supports my bottom from beneath.

"Hurry up, you're heavier than you look," says Dan, swaying slightly.

"Thanks a lot. And you're not as strong as you look, wimp-bag," I whisper back.

The top window pushes open easily. The opening is tighter than it looked from the ground and I'm regretting wearing Hanna's ridiculously chunky jumper and a gilet for this spot of cat burgling. Now I get why they wear figure-hugging catsuits in *Mission Impossible* movies.

Dan shoves me from behind and I land with an inelegant thud on the floor of the office, knocking the cushions off the window seat on my way past. I pull the torch from my gilet pocket and scan the room. I am so *Mission Impossible* now, taking a mental snapshot so I can return everything to its original position before leaving. Dan's peering in through the glass, misting it with his breath and I wave at him and do the scuba divers' OK sign with my thumb and index finger.

The big filing cabinet is locked. Dr Harrison must

be taking patient confidentiality way more seriously since Ramesh Desai's visit. I check his desk drawers carefully, looking for any small key. In the bottom one I find the whisky bottle, cigarettes and mouth spray.

The books on his shelf have been moved since my last visit. I pull them out one by one and a key falls out of Proust. It opens up the cabinet and I quickly thumb through the file dividers. But there's nothing relating to me filed under 'J–K', 'W–Z' or anywhere in the drawers. I've seen my file often enough in the counselling sessions – and I read it that night when the files were all over the place. It's a buff cardboard folder with my name printed on a label in the top right-hand corner of the front edge and a doodle of a spider in the bottom corner. So where's he put it?

I remember Harrison and his nervous twitchiness about the whole hypnosis procedure. He cast a glance at the window when talking about my notes. I'd assumed he was checking no one was outside and able to hear us. But maybe it was more than that. I shine the torch over the window seat where I knocked off the cushions and tap the wood. It's hollow, made from tongue-and-groove cladding. As I work my way along the front, pressing the panels, I hear a click and two of them swing open, revealing a bunch of papers. The top one's my folder and I quickly scan what's inside. He's taken notes on what I said under hypnosis and in all the other counselling sessions. I remove the sheets of paper, ready to burn them later, and tuck them inside my gilet.

The second folder has no label. Inside, clipped neatly together, are photos of Hanna, smiling out at me, together with handwritten notes of his sessions with her. Why's he hiding this? He should have passed it all to the coroner when she died. But there's one more thing I don't expect to find: Hanna's make-up bag, which was taken from my trunk. It was Harrison rooting through my private stuff.

I check the contents and read the scrappy notes in her file. No wonder he wanted the bag. He's more messed-up than I realized. There's a black-edged correspondence card and envelope tucked at the back. Just like the one *he* must have left at the shrine: *I know you didn't jump* written with his fancy pen in some mad gesture to Hanna. The card was never anything to do with me but everything to do with Dr Harrison and Hanna. And him trying to deal with what he'd done, with how he'd let her down. With guilt.

I replace everything else exactly as I found it. The door's locked so I have to make an undignified exit from the window again, using the window seat to reach up. I land like a terrible dance partner in Dan's arms, pushing him to the ground.

"Found what you wanted?" he asks, helping me up.

"Yes," I say, patting my pocket. *And more.*

36

There's a pressing need to assist sufferers of PTSD to live
with the terrible things they have experienced. But could
that also assist the perpetrators to live with the terrible
things they have done? The emotion 'shame' serves a
useful purpose as a moral check on our actions. Even if
we could do so, should we erase it?

    Bridge, L. (2014) 'The Moral Memory Maze'
Cognitive Neuroscientist Review, *Vol 2, no 7, p.18*

It's late. Harrison's briefing went on and on. I borrow
Lena's lighter and burn the pages from my 'counselling'
file outside on the terrace while the others are sorting
out hot chocolates. I slip back inside the Common
Room before I'm missed.

"I could feel the life blood draining from me," Dan
says. "That's two hours of my life I'll never see again."

"Doing bearings and trig points is not my favourite
way to spend an evening," I say.

"Harrison went on about health and safety too
much," says Keira. "He's obsessed. Staying in pairs,

taking on water, first aid, keep out of the bogs. Some people looked terrified by the time he'd finished. I'm glad I'm only being a marshal."

"And that bizarre bit at the end when he went all teary: 'I'd never forgive myself if anything happened to any of you on my watch'," says Maya, imitating Harrison.

That's what guilt does to you.

"It doesn't look good if someone you're counselling dies, like Hanna did," says Keira.

"And Barker can't afford to lose any other staff, after Desai's disappearance," adds Dan.

"That's all *so* not our problem," says Maya, clapping her hands together. "We need to change the vibe for this event after his downer and luckily I bring good news: the T-shirts have finally arrived. They're so cool. I was going to save them for tomorrow but we all need cheering up." She drags a cardboard box out from under the table-tennis table. "Choose a baggy size and then you can wear it over your other layers otherwise you won't have it on show."

"Wow. They're bright! Do we need to wear sunglasses?" says Dan.

"They are more neon than I'd expected," says Maya. "But at least we won't lose each other if it's foggy."

"I'll take one to Harrison," I say, grabbing an extra large. After what I saw in his office, I want to talk to him on my own. "Won't be long. I'll see you all later if you're still here, or in the morning, ready for action."

Dan looks up, puzzled, but I dash off before he can say anything, leaving him to Keira, who's enjoying trying different shirt sizes against his torso.

*

I knock gently on the door to Mandela Lodge but don't wait for an answer. Harrison's sitting at his desk, his head in his hands. He barely looks up. "Jess. What can I do for you?"

I pull up a chair.

He adjusts his glasses and rubs his hands through his thinning hair. "Now isn't such a good time. Maybe tomorrow. We'll all feel better after the hike's over."

"I don't think you're going to feel any better," I say.

"Me? I meant you."

"You're the one who looks like death warmed up."

"Thanks." He smiles for the first time.

"I brought you a gift," I say, handing over the T-shirt. "We can all look ridiculous together tomorrow."

"Walking together to remember," he reads.

Too much remembering is eating both of us up.

"Tonight is a new kind of counselling session," I say. "Two-way. You know my secrets and I know yours."

He shifts on his chair. "I don't know what on earth you mean. If you're talking about the other night when I'd had a little too much to drink..."

More than a little, but I let it pass.

I swallow and then I say it: "I'm not talking about that. I mean Hanna."

I've got his attention. He looks me straight in the eyes.

I carry on: "And the drugs you were 'prescribing', illegally."

He starts to deny it, but really what's the point? He knows I saw her medication. I realize I *told* him in our memory box conversation. He was worried enough to go to my room to retrieve them. He slumps defeated in the chair before sighing and finally saying: "I was trying to help her. Really. She was insecure in many ways."

"Even though she was beautiful."

"She couldn't see that herself, sadly. But when all's said and done, she was just a kid." Harrison sighs and pours us each a glass of water. "I've given up the hard stuff, again. I'm trying to be a better person, to others, to my wife, if she'll let me."

"So you were giving Hanna medicine you got online," I say. "I read her file."

He raises an eyebrow.

"Don't worry, I've left it where I found it," I say. "And I'm not going to tell anyone."

"It seems stupid now," he says. "But at the time … I wanted to help her anxieties. I thought I was, I don't know…"

"Able to fix her? The only one able to fix her."

"Which shows what a terrible grasp I had of my role as her counsellor," he says, shaking his head. "I was keeping her to myself, not referring her to a proper clinical psychologist or psychiatrist. God complex, narcissistic personality disorder, counter-transference – you name it, I had it. Textbook breaches. And I've violated every code of the British Psychotherapy and Counselling Council to boot."

"So our little episode with hypnotherapy…" I say.

"…is merely the icing on the cake of my unethical adventures."

"Well, here's to that," I say, raising my glass. "Don't worry, I was never taken in by your certificates from dodgy institutions. I'm assuming your 'doctor' one wouldn't get you a job anywhere that they check these things out properly."

We both sip our water. Harrison swirls his glass like it's a gin and tonic, as though there's an answer hidden in the bottom of it.

"The guilt," says Harrison. "I can't shake it off. I gave her medication which I had no authority to prescribe. I've been living in fear that someone will come and say they found traces in the tests they did on her."

"That's why I scared the living daylights out of you the other day talking about drug testing?" I ask.

"Yes. So I added burglary to my list of misdemeanours."

"You weren't very good at it," I say.

"I've come to realize I'm not very good at anything. Except messing up." He takes a gulp of water again. He looks older. A grey and lined middle-aged loser.

"So the combination of these drugs you gave her…?" I ask.

"They had a bad mix of side effects which I should have monitored."

"And she was mixing them with alcohol," I say. "She'd had a boozy summer with Ed and she carried on when term started. She mixed cocktails in our room. She called them cocktails but they were mostly vodka, with a paper umbrella. And she lived on caffeine drinks." *I encouraged her.*

"I should have realized. I should have been keeping a better eye on her. Confusion and weight loss…"

"Plus blurred vision, tachycardia, nausea," I say. "But you can't know for sure what happened that day she fell from the window, can you?"

"No, but this feeling in the pit of my stomach tells me I'm responsible. I'm quitting for good," he says. "Not fit to practise anything. I'm resigning straight after Hanna's Hike. No doubt the Principal will want to hush it up. But I wanted to do one last thing for Hanna before I go. I thought I'd feel better."

"Maybe you should get some counselling?" I say. "It's tragic when young life full of promise is ripped away but time can heal." I repeat the fortune-cookie psychology from his sessions back to him.

"Physician, heal thyself!"

"I'm not going to tell anyone," I say. "I meant what I said."

"Thank you. My wife's putting it all down to a midlife crisis. I haven't persuaded her to let me move back in yet. Another area of my life I seem to have messed up."

We sit in silence for a moment. I don't want to embark on marriage counselling.

"I'm missing the biscuits," I say. "I miss the custard

creams and the chocolate digestives."

"I thought you hated everything about our sessions," he says. "You're one of my more challenging clients."

"There's a lot going on in my head," I say.

"And you were always holding back. Confession is good for the soul. If there's anything you need to tell me?"

Should I tell him and then both our souls are cleansed?

I take a breath. "Sometimes I liked Hanna, sometimes I hated her."

"That's the first honest statement you've made to me about your relationship with Hanna," he says. "But that can be friendship at your age: love/hate. She played games with people's feelings. Keira, for instance. She's reacted most strangely to Hanna's death, harboured a most unhealthy fixation. Writing sympathy cards, hanging round the shrine."

So Keira's definitely the one messing with the shrine and the Ouija board. Sick.

"I know Hanna taunted *you* about Ed. I wondered if you were jealous because of your feelings for him…" He pauses and leans forwards. "Or because of your feelings for Hanna?"

"Very Sigmund Freud of you," I say.

"It's an interesting theory, though."

"I guess that's the kind of puzzle you're meant to untangle," I say, dodging his question.

"Yes. If I was any good at my job."

I let him have a brief wallow in self-pity without correcting him. I suppose he's the nearest thing I have to a confessor, a confidant, who cannot judge me. "What if I acted on those feelings?" I say slowly. "What if I made her worse?"

Harrison looks surprised for the first time. "What? Legal highs? Ecstasy? I worried she was taking something else."

"She may well have been, but no, not from me," I say. "But I encouraged her to think about her looks all the time. I didn't stop her from messing about with laxatives, appetite suppressants, bogus diet remedies. I was pleased she wasn't the one in control for once."

I've said it now. I wait for his reaction. He says nothing.

"At the time, with Ed and everything," I say. "I wanted to get back at her. I couldn't let it go."

"But then combined with the anxiety medication I gave her…" he says.

"And the alcohol."

"She was confused and fell?" he asks.

Had the things I'd said, whispered in her ear like poison, made her feel so bad that she'd wanted to jump? I think of her on that last day. She was sitting cross-legged on the bed, staring at her face in a small mirror, pulling at the flesh across her cheekbones. Dark, dark shadows under her eyes. I was angry that she was doing this to herself. I said she looked terrible, had let herself go. "Ed will be better off without you," I said. "We'd all be better off without you." And then I slammed our door shut behind me and didn't ever see her again. Alive, that is.

I say quietly: "Or maybe she actually wanted to kill herself?"

"I don't believe that. She'd never said so. But given we've established I'm a terrible counsellor, I'm not the best judge."

"I think you're doing OK with me tonight," I say.

There's a hint of a smile at the corner of his mouth.

"So there we are," I say. "Did you cause what happened to Hanna, or did I, or the vodka cocktails or Hanna's anxiety? Or was it breaking up with Ed that was a tipping point? Or was it all just a terrible accident?"

Dr Harrison stands up and walks to the window. "It's impossible to say. We'll never know the truth of it.

It seems we all have our own versions of the past. Our own remembered history."

I stand next to him and we both look out at the courtyard. There's a twinkling of candles from the shrine, as if Hanna wants to join the conversation.

"These last few weeks have been hell," he says, wiping his eyes. "At times I thought she was haunting me."

"A series of unintended consequences with everyone and no one to blame. An open verdict," I say. I want to believe that it wasn't me. That it wasn't what I said. That I can change for the future. "I miss her," I whisper. "I actually miss her." I do. I really do. As I start to cry real tears I feel a release of some kind. That recurring memory of Hanna smashed on the concrete is being filed on a shelf in my mind-library. Harrison's tissue box is empty but he gives me a creased handkerchief. He holds me while I shake and weep. And afterwards I realize that talking with Harrison has finally made me feel better.

37

*Try the following memory exercise: Read each word
once. Close the book and write down as many as you can
remember:*

candle	*flowers*
soft toys	*Lego*
guilt	*shame*
love	*betrayal*

Work Your Memory

It's cold in the courtyard. My breath hangs in the
air and my nose tingles. But I'm feeling better about
Hanna.

I pick up her weathered photo by the shrine and
touch her cheek through the glass. Barker had a major
tidy up after the Halloween excesses, but I wring out
the last two teddy bears and add them to the rubbish
with the burnt-down candles and the bedraggled
flowers. I gather up the remaining candle holders and
cards. I check the writing. Harrison was right: I reckon
most of them are written by Keira. If she had her way,

this would be here forever. No doubt it was Keira who set up the shrine on Halloween to spook me, who moved the planchette around the Ouija board. Her macabre fun and games are over.

In the chapel, I pick up the Book of Condolence, sitting lonely on a side table, unopened for days, and add it to the rest of the artefacts in a spare cardboard box. Finally, I dismantle the Hanna Carlsen collaborative peace model. It's a multicoloured abstract with Lego figures incongruously smiling out from random windows. The figure with a moustache looks strangely sinister.

I write on the top of the box: 'To be sent to the Carlsen Family'. I'm sure Hanna's family have had their fill of all this too. Mawkish sentiment from people like Keira who didn't love Hanna like they did. Like I did. One more day tomorrow and then I can put this to rest. I can say goodbye.

I don't really expect anyone to still be there, but when I return to the Common Room, Dan's watching TV, flipping beer mats on the edge of the table.

"Hey, you," I say. "Shove up." I lean my head against his shoulder, breathing in the smell of him.

"Glad you came back for me," he says. "I wasn't sure you would. Where've you been?"

"Tidying up," I say. "Tidying up and sorting out."

"You look knackered," he says. "You need a fifteen-mile hike tomorrow in bad weather to perk you up."

"Can't wait. Team Dan and Jess. Yay!"

"I thought we were Team Jess and Dan. That was the rule you set. Along with no mushy stuff." He smiles at me. "When's the next meeting of the Memory Club?"

"We've got enough to be going on with," I say. "I need to think about what to do with it all. How to get Coleman back. Maybe prepare material to send to the press, her university, scientific journals."

I don't tell Dan – he wouldn't understand – but my revenge on Coleman is going to be a lot more dramatic than sending a letter to a newspaper. She's responsible for my mum's death, however she chooses to dress it up. And if she wants me back on the Programme, back to being the girl with the amazing memory, the only way to stop that other than running forever is to get the proof of what she's really about and expose her. Or do I have to stop her in another, more permanent way? After Callum and what happened to Lena, I need to be prepared. I can't rely on Ramesh Desai to come and save me. I'm doing the hike for Hanna and then what? Will I have to leave everything here? *Everyone?*

Dan switches off the TV. "Come on, I'll walk you

home. Coleman should be worried. You can be quite terrifying, you know. Every now and then a little ruthless look appears in your eyes, in a very attractive way." He puts his arm round me as we go back to C-Block, tiptoeing past the houseparents' apartment.

In my room, we loiter by the door, kissing. Neither of us wants to be the one to say the last goodnight.

"When this thing with Coleman's over, what's next?" he asks. "Maybe we could travel next summer. Together. If you wanted to. It's OK if not, I mean…"

This is when I feel most for him: when I can see the tiny freckles on his nose crinkle with uncertainty, when he's so damn sweet but hot and wanting to be with *me*. The girl he knows as Jess with all her weirdness.

But will it ever 'be over' with Coleman unless I put an end to it? Dan is naïve about how things are going to pan out. And yet … there *are* things I want to do. I want to get fully detoxed from whatever stuff they were pumping into me, be able to sleep easily again. Live an alternate reality. Is there any harm in indulging the fantasy that I can be 'normal'? Just for tonight?

"I'd love to travel with you," I say. "After exams, let's do it."

"We should make a list," says Dan. "A bucket list. Put places on it we want to visit."

"New York," I say quietly. "I want to take Mum to New York."

"That's settled, then. First on our list. We'll go." He takes both my hands in his. "I know you've had it really rough – with your mum and then Hanna. But things are going to get better. I'm going to make them better. You can come to stay with us at Christmas – it's hectic obviously with Dad doing services and we have waifs and strays at the vicarage as well as the uncles and aunts and cousins and Granny Mel."

He carries on while I listen in a pleasant haze of imagining whether it can be that simple – can I plop into his ready-made perfect life? A new waif and stray at the vicarage to eat mince pies and sing carols around the tree.

"The only thing is…"

Here we go. The catch. There's always a catch with the good stuff.

"You're going to need a Christmas jumper," he says. "A truly tasteless one."

He laughs and envelops me in those huge arms of his and blows a raspberry on my neck and I catch myself feeling free and happy and not locked in my mind-library. Is it possible to forget after all?

We tumble on to the bed, whacking my knee and his

elbows on the clunky bed frame. These beds were not made for two.

"Do you think they picked the bed that was least likely to lead to any form of rumpy-pumpy?" says Dan.

"Rumpy-pumpy! What are you – a retired colonel from the 1930s?"

"That is exactly what I am," he says. "I've been meaning to tell you."

We dissolve into giggles which turn into snorts and I'm remembering times when I've felt like this before. It's *joy*. Before Coleman took me on to the Programme and messed with my head.

"I don't want you to go tonight," I say, before I can stop myself. "I want you to stay." And I do. More than anything.

Dan scrunches over beside me on the bed and kisses me, his hands moving up and down my back. "I don't want to go either," he says. "Let's hope there's not a room inspection. I'm not going to fit in your cupboard."

I slot so easily into the crook of his arm with my head on his chest. I enjoy the warmth of him against my cheek, and the rise and fall of his breathing. I've had all these terrible feelings of hate and jealousy and regret and fear and guilt bouncing around in me for so long, it's hard to give in to intimacy and caring about someone and letting them care about me. Being vulnerable. I take his hand and knot my fingers through his and he strokes my palm with his thumb.

He pulls at my top and we fumble with my skinny jeans. Whoever thought they were a good idea? I feel my way through his layers, littering the floor with cast-off clothing, until I find warm skin. We've stopped laughing, become quieter, more intense. I can finally let go.

I've been living inside my head too long, thinking too much about the dead. Time to join the living.

*

I wake. I see the glowing light of a phone. Dan's sitting up in the chair by the window scrolling away, checking Facebook or something lame like that. Or is he sexting? He's never come clean on the 'someone special' who gave him the fancy watch. I sigh and yawn to make him realize I can see what he's doing. I stretch out in what I think is an irresistible way so he'll come back to bed. But he looks up guiltily and ruins everything. Mystery solved – sexting not texting. Keira? Why else would he be doing it at four in the morning?

"Sorry. I was, er." He hastily taps at it. "I'll switch it off." But not before I clock the colour. Bright orange.

He was on my phone, not his.

I sit up and reach over for it. "What are you doing with my phone?" I look at the screen. No calls made, no texts sent. I look at the browser but he's cleared the history. I can't tell what he was looking at. He squeezes back beside me, his feet like ice. He kisses my bare shoulder, travels his hands over my thighs. "Shush, come and play with me." He pulls the duvet up over our heads and kisses me.

"But why were you…" I say weakly.

"I was checking the news app, that's all. Chill. Mine's completely out of charge. I should've asked but I didn't want to wake you." He holds my face in his hands and kisses it inch by inch. "You were lying there so bewitchingly, snuffling like a hedgehog, hogging the duvet, arms splayed out like you own this single bed." He kisses me again on the lips but his words have already diffused my anger. I must learn to trust more, not to think the worst.

And then I spot over his shoulder that his phone is still blinking away, plugged in on the bedside table. It's charged.

He lied.

And my heart goes cold.

38

Remember, remember the fifth of November.

Traditional rhyme

I dive from the side in a flurry of bubbles and hold my breath. I glide, skimming over the mosaic below. My lungs are screaming for air as I finally break the surface. My mind's racing. All the bad stuff's back. What an idiot I was – thinking that Dan was actually interested in me, falling for him. Falling in love with him.

As soon as he fell back asleep, I grabbed his room key. Felix was crashed out snoring heavily, the duvet pulled over his head, as I tiptoed around their room. It didn't take me long to find out what I needed to know.

Dan knew Hanna.

He has a photo of her tucked inside his bedside drawer. Hanna on a beach, blowing a kiss at the camera, her chunky jumper hanging loose, her white-blond hair streaming behind her. Looking like a soft-focus shampoo advert. On the back she'd written: 'Best day! Hannie xxx.' And on her wrist – it's Dan's watch. The one he said was from 'someone special'.

I count the lengths until I get to fifty and my body's crying out for a rest. The physical exhaustion gives me something else to feel. I do a whole length underwater until my lungs are bursting again.

I pull myself on to the side and lie spread-eagled on the cold, tiled floor while goose pimples slowly cover my skin. There's no one in the world who actually cares whether I catch pneumonia and die. In fact, that seems a good option at the moment. *I* don't even care whether I catch pneumonia and die. Tears roll down my cheeks, pooling in my ears, and soon they give way to sobs. No one can hear me. I can remember all the other times I've cried, colliding in a mess of terrible memories. Once you open up and replay those scenes, it's a flood of raw emotion. I've been keeping a tight, tight lid on it for so long. The feelings are overwhelming. Why am I cursed with this memory? Why does it have to spoil my every waking moment with the weight of all that's passed? I thought Dan was someone I could share it with, but I'm wrong again. He's made a fool of me. Like Hanna and Ed did. Unrequited love is a bad emotion to have on endless repeat.

I'm not even any good at freezing to death. I'm too cold and shivery. I wrap myself in the towel and dry my eyes. I imagine Mum telling me to pull myself together, that I'm *her* daughter so act like it. No point crying over things you cannot change.

I get dressed and, in a clear, logical way, review my time with Dan, slotting in each scene. He was always asking questions about Hanna; he knew her pet name was Hannie; he knew her jumper though I'd never told him it was hers; he completely lost it when he realized he was in Hanna's bedroom at the seance. I could go on. I've been so busy looking for clues to something else, thinking he was helping me. All the time, he wanted to know what happened to Hanna. 'You can always talk to me', trips to the shrine, the vigil. All that pretending. All that lying through his teeth. And checking though my phone. Looking for what? Photos of Hanna? A confession?

Dan was playing me. I was an idiot to think he

cared. Why would he? Why would someone as good-looking as Dan, with so much going for him, be attracted to me? Jess the sulky one, the introvert, the weirdo. Especially when he could have Keira, beautiful Barbie doll Keira who's been throwing herself at him for weeks now. Who would resist that unless he had a bigger plan to execute?

Maya said it was all moving too quickly. Of course it was. I should have listened to her. She was trying to be a friend and warn me. Dan couldn't hook up with me fast enough. And I let him.

And I shared things with him. Not only the physical intimacy, though my flesh crawls now at the thought of it, but I told him personal things about Mum, the Programme. I sliced open my brain and heart and laid them bare for him to stamp on. All that time he was pretending to help me, he was only interested in Hanna.

The college community's beginning to come to life. The groundsmen are fighting a losing battle, trying to clear the paths with the leaf-blower. Others are piling branches on to the bonfire down on the terraced lawn, ready for tonight. Dr Harrison raises a hand in greeting. He's in his marshal's kit already and checking equipment off on his clipboard. He looks better today, like he finally has a purpose on his last day at Dartmeet.

I head back to my room and cautiously open the door. Dan's gone. Thank goodness. He's left a note on the pillow:

Hope swim was refreshing. See you after breakfast, ready to rock Dartmoor.

Dan xxx

I scrunch it into a tiny ball. I take the earrings he gave me from my jewellery box. They seem sinister now when days ago I thought them quirkily romantic. What a fool. I get the symbolism now of giving me a *memento mori*. He was showing *he* hadn't forgotten Hanna, and I shouldn't either. The tiny skulls are laughing at me. I close my fist around them and throw them against the wall. The glass cracks and one of the tiny hourglasses falls, skidding across the floor. I pick up the broken pieces and throw them in the bin where they belong, along with my so-called relationship with Dan.

But then I notice more correspondence.

A new postcard with the familiar view of Gara Stone Circle is caught on the rug, as though it's been posted under the door. The fifth card from the pack. The final one. It says:

REMEMBER, REMEMBER THE FIFTH OF NOVEMBER

Ramesh Desai just can't resist his last gasp of drama.

I look at the laminated map Dr Harrison handed round, with its neat arrows showing directions and distances. The timing's possible. I commit the map to memory and work out where I need to diverge from the hike route to get to the stone circle.

The only thing holding me here was Dan and now that relationship is shattered into pieces like the earrings. As the card says, it's the fifth of November. A day for treason and plot. Betrayal. And for fireworks.

39

O, what a tangled web we weave when first we practise to deceive.

'Marmion' – Sir Walter Scott

Once I'm dressed in all my walking layers, I pull on the neon Hanna's Hike T-shirt. As I lace up my boots, memories of the trip to Ashburton flood in: dancing around the charity shop, Dan's arm round my waist. All false. That day has changed forever.

Are my memories real or imagined, genuine or doctored? How can I sort the truth from the lies, honesty from deceit?

*

Dan's with the other walkers outside doing the final

checks on his rucksack, as though all is normal, joking with Keira. Of course *she* would be there, waiting to pounce on any unattended boyfriend. He sees me standing across the terrace and waves. His face lights up as our eyes lock. His warm and twinkling, and mine – not so much. Before he can react, Maya grabs me and pulls me to the podium. She looks like she's joined the army, in full camo gear with a stripe of paint on each cheek. The camouflage look is slightly ruined by the neon T-shirt.

Principal Barker takes the loudhailer and welcomes us all in a crackle of feedback. "Today, we meet in a spirit of remembrance, friendship and love of the great outdoors. We're here at the suggestion of our own students." She turns towards me and Maya. Maya squeezes my hand. Keira looks happier to stay at Dan's side rather than push through the crowd to join us. "And of course," continues Barker, "thanks are due to our own resident Bear Grylls, Dr Harrison."

He does an awkward bow to a smattering of applause. Has he handed in his letter of resignation yet, or will he just disappear during the day?

Barker continues: "As you know, one of our community died tragically: Hanna Carlsen." Hanna's name echoes round the grounds, travelling across the gardens out and on to the moor. "So as you're walking together to remember Hanna, also remember the need to look after each other, to be kind, to speak up when we're worried about one of our community. That's the best kind of legacy for Hanna." She pauses for a solemn moment of reflection, head bowed. Maya wipes away a tear.

"We wish all our walkers well and look forward to welcoming you back here for a bonfire supper and fireworks," says Barker, raising her arms as though she's blessing us in some hippy-dippy way, her rainbow-coloured scarf waving in the breeze.

The mist shows no sign of lifting with no sunshine to break it up. There's not much time before our departure slot and I need to make it to Gara Stones for noon. I didn't get much sleep, so I stoke up on caffeine at the catering tent. I wait for Dan to join me. He greets me like nothing bad has happened. Like he hasn't betrayed me. I can't stand the hypocrisy of it all.

At first he's smiling but then he sees me glaring back at him, my ill-hidden anger.

"Let's not pretend any more," I say.

Confusion's written all over his face. He's very good at lying, at pretending. "What? I haven't a clue what you're talking about."

"Did you find what you wanted on my phone, Dan?"

"I, er." He shifts his weight from foot to foot.

He's so busted. He hasn't even got a poxy excuse to throw back at me. I force my hands into fists to stop them shaking.

"OK. Here goes." He licks his lips nervously and clears his throat. "I wanted to see if you had any photos."

"Of Hannie?"

He blushes.

I've caught him out. Too easy. "Because they wouldn't be of me, would they?" I say. "I don't do photos, you know that. Those ones Maya took at Halloween when you can barely tell it's me, they're my first photos for ages."

"Yes, OK. I woke up. You were fast asleep. I thought I'd have a quick look to see if you have any photos of Hanna and Ed."

"To perv over them, or what?"

For the first time, he laughs. "Definitely not. Ed's my cousin."

My mouth literally drops open. "What?"

"Ed's my cousin. My aunt's son."

"I know what a cousin is even though I don't have any, thank you." I sound petulant, like an angry eight-year-old. His aunt's son, so they have different surnames. I look at the shape of Dan's face. He'd looked slightly familiar to me when we first spoke and now I get why.

"Ed and Hanna were inseparable in the summer holidays so I saw a lot of her too," he says.

"Stop with the lies," I say. "I found the photo. The one you keep hidden next to your bed. "Best day! Hannie. Kiss, kiss, kiss."

"You've searched my room? Unbelievable. That day on the beach in the photo, Ed was there, all the family was there. We played beach cricket and had a barbecue. Ed took a photo of Hanna in that Danish jumper and she sent it to us. It was a thank-you for a good day out, welcoming her." He sighs. "I was always due to start at Dartmeet but I was ill at the beginning of term and joined later, after … Hanna. Ed had already left, too shaken up to stay. I promised him that I'd see if I could shed any light on why, *if*, Hanna would do something like that, kill herself. Ed felt guilty because he'd broken up with her. Guilty that he hadn't stopped it somehow. He thought people felt it was his fault."

I was part of that impression.

"I didn't exactly lie about being his cousin – nobody asked me," he says. "And I thought people would be more likely to tell me about the real Hanna if they didn't know my connection to Ed."

I kick at the gravel with my clumpy walking boots. "Or you could sneak around like Hercule Poirot poking your nose into our lives and getting information under false pretences."

"You've been snooping in *my* room to find the photo, remember."

"*After* you went through my phone," I say. "No way does that make us quits."

"But once you and I *happened*, it was too late to say anything about knowing Ed," he says. "I knew you'd hate it. The lie grew and grew."

"All the more reason to tell me, to come clean."

"And you tell *me* everything, do you?" He frowns. "Because I think you're holding back on quite a lot."

I definitely haven't told him everything. Not my real name, not about the postcards, or Desai, or Callum. It's a long list.

And definitely not what I did to Hanna. How can I tell him now about how I hated Hanna for going out with Ed? How disappointed I was that her plan to invite me back to Denmark for the summer was dropped in a heartbeat for her to spend time making sandcastles with him. Can I tell him that I don't even think she liked Ed that much at the beginning, that it was just another game for her of picking people up and dropping them? She did it with Keira all the time. Best friend/not best friend. Linking arms with her and paying her compliments one day, then blanking her the next. The friendship game. She did it with everyone, especially me.

"What about the watch in the photo?" I say. "Your watch from 'someone special'?"

"The watch was a birthday present from Granny Mel. Hanna was wearing it to keep it safe while I was surfing. She was the only one not in and out of the sea. That's all." Dan chuckles, which makes me even madder. "Don't tell me you're jealous of my granny!"

"How convenient," I say sarcastically. "Roll out the little old lady story."

"For goodness' sake. Have you heard yourself? I'd thought Ed must be wrong about you. He thought you'd said something mean to Hanna about her weight, her looks."

Ed's right. I made sure she felt terrible about herself.

"Have a good briefing session on me, did you?" I say. "Are you phoning him regularly with updates?"

"No. Not at all," says Dan. "Look, you can believe me or not about the photo. And the watch. Phone Ed. He'll tell you."

"He hates me apparently. Why would he talk to me?"

"No, I didn't mean… Oh, you are the most infuriating person I have ever met. I've been *helping* you, remember."

"Yes. So, so helpful," I say. "Making yourself so indispensable, when all the time you were snooping. Maybe you're even working for the Programme."

He shakes his head. "You're so paranoid."

"Stop acting like you're the victim here. It's *you* who's been spying on *me*, lying and pretending that you like me."

"I do like you. More than like you. Last night we…" He tries to touch me but I pull away.

"You have a weird way of showing it. You've manipulated me into falling in…" The words catch in my throat. "…into having feelings for you. So if anyone has the moral high ground, it's me, not you." My voice has got louder. People are staring. The catering assistant serving the teas and coffees is transfixed, holding a milk jug, like we're the entertainment for the day. A full soap-opera performance. But I don't care. I can't stay around here anyway if Coleman's so close to working out where I am. I don't know what I was thinking, indulging in some stupid fantasy life where I could carry on here, with Dan. I'm best back on my own, relying on myself alone.

He looks crushed, hurt. "If you still want to be on a team with me as planned, we're due to leave in ten minutes. It's up to you." He slings his rucksack over his shoulder and walks off, not looking back.

The catering assistant turns back hurriedly to her tea urn, eyes down as though she hasn't been enjoying listening to the show, while I help myself to another coffee. Do I believe Dan? He's always so plausible. A well-oiled lying machine. And yet, my memories of last night come back – the feelings I had for him. The feelings I thought I saw in him. It felt real. It feels real now.

"Lovers' tiff this morning?" says Keira, appearing at my side, barely able to contain her smirk. "I do hope you've not split up," she says, looking at me keenly. "Everyone said that you two didn't have much in common but … anyway I'm here for you if you've been dumped."

"You'd like that, wouldn't you?" I say. "Have some self-respect. Stop throwing yourself at someone else's boyfriend."

Keira reddens. "I don't know what you mean."

"Yeah, right. Cut it out, Keira. And you can cut the drama too. No more anonymous candle-lighting and dramatic music. You're not going to use the memory of my friend Hanna any more to get some sick Goth kick out of her death. No more Book of Condolence mystery entries. No more messages from 'beyond the grave'. Nothing. It's over. Go and talk that one over with a new counsellor. I'm going on this crappy hike."

I leave Keira there, opening and closing her mouth like the vapid goldfish she is.

40

Remember, remember the fifth of November
Gunpowder, treason and plot.
I see no reason why such terrible treason should ever
be forgot.

Traditional rhyme

"Where now?" says Dan.

"What?"

"I'm not speaking in a deep, metaphorical way about our relationship. I want to know which direction to walk in. I don't want to get lost." He holds the compass and we stare at it as the needle stabilizes. He folds out the map and carefully places the compass, looking up to find a landmark. "The mist's too thick. You can't see anything. We need another bearing."

"Don't we need to know where we are exactly in the first place?"

We've walked too quickly, not paying attention to the path. Being so angry with each other made us move faster. But I have to make that rendezvous with Desai at the Gara Stone Circle. I want to get out of this whole mess.

"Can't you use your memory for something useful for a change?" says Dan, jolting me out of my thoughts.

"It all looks the same at the moment – foggy. I'm not psychic," I snap back.

"So more fallibility. Careful or you'll end up average like the rest of us," he says.

"I never said I was perfect. Quite the opposite." I stop and take a drink of water, wiping my mouth on the back of my hand.

Dan adjusts my hat, pulling it down over my ears. "Keep warm," he says, his hands lingering on my head. The kind of show of affection I find hard to accept, or believe. I shrug him off. He looks hurt and I feel a pang of regret. Briefly. This is his fault. *He* betrayed *me*.

"I've been thinking since reading that memory book you lent me, and I've worked out what you're missing," he says. "We talked about it on our first date."

I wince. "You mean Ashburton? Which I now realize was a surveillance mission."

He ignores my dig. "You know what's squeezed out after all that brain capacity is taken up by you remembering *everything*?"

"Great. You've psychoanalyzed me. What's your conclusion?" I glare at him, challenging him to call it how it is.

"Empathy. You're low on empathy," he says.

"You mean I don't give a damn about other people? Boo hoo." He's right of course. But it's not news to me. I think of all the people I've deliberately hurt or pushed away while on or since the Programme.

"I wouldn't say that exactly. And we can work on it."

"Patronizing git," I say, the anger surging through me. "And empathy is exceedingly overrated."

"I think Coleman messed with your mind with her cognitive vaccine and that deep down there's the real Jess," he says, holding out his hand, which I ignore. "And I really like her."

"You don't know me at all." *The real me, what I'm capable of.* "Memories make us who we are. They shape us. Maybe mine are too bad to ever get over. Have you psychoanalyzed that? I'm damaged. Beyond repair."

"No one's beyond redemption," he says.

"Forgive me, Father, for I have sinned. You sound like Daddy the vicar. Am I your pitiable salvation project? Are you trying to save me, Dan? Because I think I'm way beyond that." I shove my hands in my pockets and stride off, Dan hurrying to catch me up. Is he right? Did Coleman make me act in a certain way, accentuate some personality traits, or is that the real, unpleasant me anyway? I'll always dwell on the past. It's so hard to let go of the personal slights and snubs, the perceived humiliations. My memory makes it impossible to be a better person. I battle it *all the time*.

We slip back into silence. All I can hear is the crunch of our boots on the path. All sound is muffled by the fog and we're in the middle of nowhere. Really the middle of nowhere.

"For someone who hates walking, you're doing pretty well," he says. He's chucking olive branches in my direction but I want to stamp all over them. What's the point in making up with him, even though my heart is pushing me to do exactly that? I'm going to have to move on again. The pleasant interlude is over. I should have gone as soon as I realized what had happened to Lena, or saw Callum, or as soon as I saw the Missing Person flyer. Dan is the one who kept me here and put me in danger.

"I'm in shape. I do swimming," I say. "I have stamina.

I can outrun you and your ridiculously heavy rucksack. Maybe we should motivate ourselves with a challenge. First one to the next checkpoint."

"Are you serious? In this weather?" he says. "I can't even see ten metres ahead."

"Well, otherwise it wouldn't be a challenge, would it?" I'm calculating, desperately looking at that map in my head and thinking of the best point to slip off towards the stone circle without Dan knowing. By the time he gets to the checkpoint and realizes I'm not there, he won't have a clue where I am. "And I need a head start," I say. "Count to three hundred really slowly. Then go. You can take my rucksack too as you're such a boy scout." Before he can complain about it, I load him up with my bag to slow him down, threading his arms through the straps so he can carry it across his front. "Start counting. One, two…"

I sprint off across the springy ground, splashing through the puddles.

"Jess, hang on! Don't be stupid! Jess!"

"Keep counting," I shout as the mist closes around me. Before I ran I'd worked out a straight line in the right direction. But now in the mist, it's hard to tell where it is. I'm looking for a tor on the horizon to get my bearings, except that there's no horizon any more.

I look back. I can't see any sign of Dan or hear him counting. His voice is lost on the moor. There's no way he'll catch me up if he sticks to the head start, and he's got both rucksacks to carry. But most of all, he doesn't know I'm now heading away from the checkpoint.

I'm looking for Bleak Cross, an ancient monument, to know where I am and where to leave the track. The atmosphere feels ghostly out here and the conditions play tricks on your senses. I swear I can hear breathing and it creeps me out. There's a solitary tree ahead, twisted and shaped by the wind. I will myself to reach it as another milestone. I jump as a pony shoots out across the path. Each of us is startled by the other. He snorts a cloud of water droplets and disappears back into the mist. I rest my hand on my heart to calm down.

At last I can make out the Celtic shape of Bleak Cross and quicken my pace. Something solid in this shifting landscape. Relieved, I lean on its weathered stone, catching my breath, feeling the worn carving beneath the grey lichen. The path forks here and I take the left one, heading gently downwards across the stony moorland, following the line of the crumbling wall of a sheepfold.

I check my watch: 11:55. Only five minutes to get to Gara Stones. I cross a small stream, swearing out loud as I slip on a stepping stone. My head's spinning with Dan. Can I trust what he says? Or is he an amazing liar who had me fooled? He loves me, he loves me not.

The rough outline of two large stones looms through the mist ahead – giant teeth poking up from the earth: Gara Stones at last. There's a small car park for visitors down the track on the other side and, beyond that, the road. There won't be any tourists in this weather. I crouch by the tallest stone, getting my breath back. It's five past twelve. The seven remaining Gara Stones drift in and out of view, revealing themselves and disappearing again as the wind carries the waves of mist. I lean round the side of the stone and look towards the path to the car park and road. No one yet. Unless I'm too late.

A whistle, long and low, like a call to a pet dog breaks the silence. Then my name. My actual name. "Freya? Freya?"

There's now a figure by the stone on the opposite side of the circle. The mist lifts slightly as the breeze gets stronger. The man's collar is turned up against the cold and he's wearing a bulky scarf but I know the silhouette; the shape of the coat. And I know the voice. The twang of a slight American accent.

Ramesh Desai. My escape route.

41

Will there be a day when we can erase bad memories and replace them with only good ones? Whoever cracks that scientific problem will have a queue of millions.

> Nash, E. (2015) 'Remembering Ethics'
> Cognitive Neuroscientist Review, *Vol 3, no 2, p.15*

"Freya, glad you made it," says Mr Desai. "Did you tell anyone else?"

"No one," I say, half-wishing I *had* told the only person who cares about me – Dan. Or maybe Maya. "And I prefer the name Jess now."

"Jess, then. We need to go." He tries to take my arm but I step back beyond his reach.

"Go where exactly? Or do you only communicate by postcard, Mr Desai?" I sit down on the cold ground and glare at him.

He squats down beside me. "I know we haven't got

off to the greatest of starts. I had your best interests at heart, but I should have spoken up sooner," he says, reaching out a hand to me. "It's important that we get out of here today. Coleman and her backers don't mess about."

I ignore his hand. "I want to expose what Coleman did to me, to my mum."

"Good, that's the spirit." He stands up, shaking out his legs. He adjusts his gloves and buttons his coat. "Though there are wider implications than what happened to you on a personal level, Jess. Terrible as that was. You're vital for her to prove her thesis and establish her cognitive vaccine, to give people the ability to forget."

I hesitantly accept his offer of a hand to help me up. "Funny, because at the moment that's what I want more than anything: to forget this whole mess."

His intense eyes look deep into mine. "Be careful what you wish for. Your memory – your own archive – is fundamental to who you are, your personal identity."

He turns to walk through the wet grass towards the track, checking I'm following him.

"Even the bad stuff?" I say.

"Especially the bad stuff. How you dealt with it has shaped you. I'm not saying it's good to suffer, but bad experiences do serve a purpose. You get burned…"

"You learn not to stick your hand in the fire?"

"Exactly. It's complex. You can't just wipe out the past without consequences, biological and ethical. Changing a response to memories to help with PTSD is one thing. But she wants to enable people to *do* terrible things with impunity. If they don't remember it, they won't feel regret, shame or horror."

He pauses and looks over his shoulder. His twitchiness is making me nervous. "Coleman's ruthless, as you're now discovering for yourself. But luckily there are people who want to stop the way her research is going." He carries on walking, faster this time, and I follow him along the path towards the car park.

"But I don't have the proof yet," I say. "I need to get hold of that so that I can make things right." *So that I can do the right thing by Mum. Get justice for her.*

"I'm here to help you," says Mr Desai. "Eventually, with your testimony…"

"But that's all it is! The testimony of a girl who says her memories have been altered," I say. "An unreliable witness by myself but Coleman wrote down data, doses, everything. Now I can see through the labyrinth of all that information. She won't throw those records away – they prove what she wants to sell."

"They've got us flights to Boston tonight," he says, checking his watch.

"Maybe if I could get into her house again or meet with her, we could record her…" I try.

"My car's down the track and we'll get going."

"Or if I…" I stop. He's not listening to me properly, to what *I* want. I can't just leave like this.

"Come on, Jess. No time to go back to the college to collect anything. I can sort everything for you. They've got you a US passport to travel on, in a new name."

But I don't budge.

Mum's box is in my room. I can't leave her there on her own. And I don't want to be a lab rat again even in a fancy facility in the States. I don't want to be studied any more.

But most of all, right now, I realize I want Dan. I can't leave Dan.

Mr Desai raises his voice. "Look, you need to see the bigger picture, Jess. They, *I*, think Coleman's work is dangerous." He's impatient with me, trying to hurry me up. "It's not just the deception, the smoke and mirrors about your mother's death."

I feel like he's holding back on the truth. "So you keep saying. Without telling me who *they* are exactly.

The way you're describing it, I'm not sure *they* do want to help me. They want to stop Coleman, sure, we have that much in common. But what am I to them? A cog? A brain on legs. Just like I was to Coleman."

"There isn't time for this now," he says, looking anxiously around him. "I can fill in the gaps – all of them, I promise. But later."

"Where's Nadia Hashimi?" I ask. "Is she on board with all this?" I trust Nadia.

He touches his face. His eyes don't meet mine, and he hesitates. The tell-tale signs of a lie. "Absolutely. Let's get going."

I've had enough of lies. Suddenly I'm too tired and cold and I want it all to stop. Mum was right about this memory of mine being a curse.

Then, out of the mist, a dark shape throws itself at Mr Desai, knocking him to the ground. I'm paralyzed, watching like it's happening somewhere else. The attacker's wearing a hood but it slips as the two figures grapple on the grass. Mr Desai's trying to roll the attacker off, and I can see one of his ears. It has a chunk missing at the top. It's Brett.

I look for something to hit him with. I grab a rock about the size of my palm and throw it at Brett as hard as I can. It hits his back with a thud.

He stops for a second, long enough for Mr Desai to roll out from under him and haul himself up. "Run, Jess. Run!" he shouts. He's trying to stand fully upright, holding his ribs. I can't leave him like this. He looks pleadingly at me again. "Get out of here," he whispers. "I'll hold him up as long as I can. Run." He tosses me the car keys and launches himself at Brett while I sprint down the track towards the car park.

The images of the fight are already replaying in my head. I run to his car, cursing myself for not starting driving lessons. But I have watched Dan drive Uja. I replay in my head, like an instructional video, the way he started the engine, checked the mirror and flicked the indicators. Mirror, signal, manoeuvre.

I press the key fob to unlock the doors. I get in the driver's seat, shaking with adrenalin. Keep calm, keep calm. The engine starts first time, unlike Uja. I can do this.

I focus in on the periphery of my memories to figure out what Dan was doing with the pedals and copy the actions. Right foot on the accelerator pedal. It revs noisily and I back off slightly. Left foot down on the clutch, first gear, find the biting point, and cautiously press on the gas, while easing up on the clutch. The car's straining to move. I release the handbrake and the car splutters forwards and stalls. I look in the rear-view mirror. I can't see any sign of Mr Desai or Brett. Yet. I try the process again, this time kangaroo-hopping the car a couple of times before I get the hang of the clutch. *Come on, come on.* It still doesn't feel right. It's not accelerating and there's a grinding noise. Something's blocking the front wheels and I get out to check. My heart sinks when I see the state of the tyres. They've been slashed. Brett's handiwork? This car's going nowhere.

I read the map in my head. I run towards the road and turn left. This links back towards the main route across the moor. I've got about six miles by road to reach Dartmeet and get Harrison, Barker, Maya, *anyone* to do something. I can't possibly run all the way. And I'm worried about Ramesh Desai. Should I have left him even though he told me to? With a sickening feeling I realize that if Brett slashed the tyres that means one thing for sure: he has a knife.

I keep on jogging, as though I'm out with the running club on a normal Saturday morning. I reach the bigger road with a stitch in my side. There's an occasional firework in the distant sky. People who can't wait until darkness and the bonfire night displays.

In the stillness I hear something. It's a vehicle.

Headlights. I take off the brightest thing I have: the neon Hanna's Hike T-shirt. *Thank you, Maya.* I stand in the middle of the road holding it above my head like I'm that girl in *The Railway Children* waving a red petticoat to stop the train. And it's working. The black Audi with tinted windows is slowing. The window opens only a few centimetres. I don't blame the driver, as I'm splattered in mud and waving my arms like a lunatic. Hitchhiking is normal round here, though you don't normally ask people to go back the way they came. I need a full charm offensive. Charm is not my strong point.

I use my jolly-hockey-sticks boarding-school voice. "Thanks so much for stopping. I'm on Hanna's Hike with Dartmeet College and I got lost and hurt my ankle. Can you please give me a lift there – it's a few miles further down the road?" I simper. "In that direction, sorry." I point back the way he's come.

"Not a problem. In you get."

The car doors lock reassuringly as I ease on to the safety of the passenger seat and do up my seat belt. The car pulls away. I've escaped. I'm safe. I let myself relax at last.

But the driver shows no sign of turning. He's speeding up. We pass a layby that's the perfect place to do a U-turn.

A passenger behind me leans forwards and places a hand on my shoulder.

"Hello, Freya. Remember me?"

42

The one who remembers most wins the game.
                    Scouting Games – Robert Baden-Powell

"This is a stroke of luck. You're not an easy girl to find," says Professor Coleman. Her voice is cold, annoyed and extremely familiar.

I say nothing. She has the same short black hair, neatly plucked eyebrows and thin, pinched face. She's dressed in a designer suit with a cream blouse and green silk scarf tied loosely around her neck. My mind's a swirling mass of memories of her, from meeting her in her office that first time, to the endless tests on the Programme, to scattering Mum's ashes from the boat, to seeing her back recede as she left for work the day

I ran away. So many. And all of those memories bring a tumbling range of emotions.

"Callum came up trumps, in the end," she says.

It's a quiet road but there *must* be another vehicle soon. Will they see me through the tinted windows if I wave at them as they pass? Will they realize I need help?

"It's all been most inconvenient," she says. "You've exposed me and the Programme to unnecessary risk, Freya. Or should I call you Jess now?" Her tone is icy. "I adore what you've done with the colour of your hair. You look so like your mother as you get older."

How dare Coleman even say her name after what she did to her?

Can I get out of a moving vehicle with locked doors? I look across at the driver. He has a bruise on his chin and a familiar tattoo on his left hand. He's the man with the skull mask who got walloped by Lena and her broomstick.

"I'm surprised to find you playing at being a normal teenager in the middle of Dartmoor," she says.

"It's very flattering but you really shouldn't have gone to all this bother," I say. "I'm not coming back to the Programme. You know, the one that doesn't exist."

She opens her mouth to speak but thinks better of

it and her lips settle into a frown.

The car turns off before the reservoir and bounces down a rough track. The mist lifts briefly, revealing Ryders Bridge ahead. The River Dart's wide and rough here. I came on a canoe activity day with Hanna and Ed shortly after I joined Dartmeet and it scared the living daylights out of me.

I picture Harrison's route map and check my watch again. Ryders Bridge is the fourth checkpoint. Given an average walking speed of three miles per hour, the first people won't be coming through for at least an hour. I shouldn't have sent Dan on a wild goose chase with both our bags.

"We're picking up an old friend of yours here," says Coleman. "All very *Hound of the Baskervilles* running around Dartmoor. How ironic that poor old Brett has had to go out in all weathers looking for you and I found you without even getting out of the car."

"I read your book," I say, to buy some time. I know she'll want to brag about it.

"Top ten non-fiction bestseller list this week," she says. "People are so interested in memory. We all have one, you see. Though some people's are better than others."

I swallow hard. "You left a lot out of the book," I

say. "The Programme, for instance."

"How nice of you to take an interest," she says. "I've written a second version containing all the missing information – *Principles of Memory* by Professor A.E. Coleman, the uncut version – in which *you* feature rather heavily but that is a rather limited edition. Limited in fact to the people who've paid for it from the start. It's been what your generation might call 'crowdfunded' through specialist channels."

The driver pulls over on a rough patch of gravel and unlocks our doors.

"Out, please," says Coleman, wrapping a pashmina around her shoulders. "My techniques may be unorthodox but they get results."

I match the landscape to the map in my head, contemplating how far I could run before the car caught me up. Or the driver.

She nods to the boot which is piled high with luggage. "They're setting me up with a beautiful research facility somewhere rather warmer and more luxurious than here."

"Not too far away, I hope," I say sarcastically.

"I won't be coming back to England. Look at the weather; it's so melancholy." She gestures around us at the misty moor. "Where I'm going has a much better view."

"Congratulations. You've become a Bond villain," I say. "Are they providing a shark tank and a fluffy white cat?"

"Hilarious," says Coleman. "You always had such an acid tongue, like your charming mother. The short answer is that they're giving me anything I want, and gold-plating it." She examines my face with her piercing gaze. "I do miss our sessions together."

"Is that why you've gone to all this effort to find me?" I say.

"Oh, Jess! Of course I wanted to say goodbye to my favourite research subject. Your brain will make my reputation and a considerable fortune." She scans the area, no doubt looking for Brett as she carries on with her lecture. "I've spent years being underappreciated, filling out endless applications for research funding, grovelling to committees who don't understand the first thing about what I'm trying to do. But finally I found private investors who could see the true possibilities in my research and point me in a particular direction to realize its full potential. And I always had you and the ultimate memory as my pièce de résistance. I couldn't have done it without you."

"I'd like to say I was happy to help but you never

really gave me the choice."

"There are always sacrifices along the way," she says. *Mum.*

"…and considerable expenses. These investors have been so useful on that front. But they want to see results, Jess, tangible results."

"Go ahead then, deliver your cognitive vaccine and all the paperwork to back it up. I'm not stopping you but I don't want to be a part of it all."

She frowns. "It seems you were paying rather more attention than I realized. But you see, my investors are not as understanding as me. There's a lot at stake in the development of this. I'm afraid you don't have a choice." She knocks on the roof of the car and the driver gets out, pulling a thin canvas case from under his seat. He stands facing us, unzipping a shotgun.

"My investors don't like loose ends," says Coleman, picking a piece of fluff from her jacket cuffs. "And they certainly don't want any evidence of what we've done left lying around for other people to benefit from – not after they put in all that money and I put in all that effort. It wouldn't be fair, Jess, would it? Anyone can see that."

The driver polishes the gun barrel and checks the chambers.

"So that's why I have to take them *all* my research materials. They are most insistent that I hand everything over." She tilts her head to one side. "And I'm so sorry, Jess, but that's why we've had to find you. Because 'everything' includes you."

43

Memories can be rebuilt on recall. We can aid this reconsolidation with a cognitive vaccine of tailored drug therapy. Thus, repeatedly prompting individuals to imagine an event that they never experienced can produce an absolute conviction of having lived that event in a significant number of participants. Even the exceptional ones.
Principles of Memory (Limited Edition) – *Professor A.E. Coleman*

"I'm not going anywhere with you," I say, in barely a whisper.

"Be a good girl and come along quietly. It'll be so much less fuss," says Coleman. "Once Brett gets here, we'll be off." She smiles as though she's promising me an outing. I'm guessing she's had some treatment, maybe Botox on her too-smooth forehead and a filler in her lips. The effect is plastic and false.

I look out across the moor in the mist, willing a hiker to appear. But there's no one. I'm picturing the map in my head, seeing Ryders Bridge and the land around it.

We're not that far as the crow flies from where I left Mr Desai and Brett. I recall in detail Dr Harrison's navigation briefing and that the blue tufted symbols on the map indicate marshy ground. On Dartmoor that means a peat bog. The better terrain lies across the stone bridge on the other side of the river.

Coleman and her driver aren't going to let me go. That much is clear. I need to improve my odds before Brett turns up and things get a whole lot worse.

"Brett's not going to get here by himself," I lie. "Last time I saw him, he was blundering about with a sprained ankle."

Her face twitches slightly in annoyance. "You didn't say you'd seen him."

"You didn't ask. Why do you think I flagged a car down?" I say. "He's even angrier than I remember him. He needs to work on that."

Coleman checks her phone then calls her driver over. The shotgun's still casually aimed in my direction. "Give that to me. You need to go and find Brett."

He looks down at his neat suit and polished shoes.

"Get on with it," she snaps. "I'm not dressed for it either."

The driver grabs a coat and a torch from the car. He's wrong if he thinks a torch is going to help him in these conditions – it makes the fog glow brighter when the light bounces back. He tucks his trousers into his socks. Those smart shoes are already ruined. His back soon disappears from view. The shouts of 'Brett! Brett!' soon fade into the gloom. He's walking straight towards the boggy mire. Exactly where I want him to go.

Even in broad daylight on a summer's day bogs on Dartmoor can be dangerous. Locals stick to the high tufts of grass like stepping stones, dodging the pools of liquid peat and the deep moss, but no one would try to cross it in these conditions. It won't be long until he gets stuck, sucked down. And if he struggles, he'll only make it worse.

Now it's just me and Coleman.

Though she does have the advantage of a rather mean-looking shotgun.

*

Coleman sits half in, half out of the driver's seat. I can tell she's not used to handling a gun. She balances it awkwardly across her lap and checks her phone again. She's so out of her comfort zone of a clinical office in London.

"No signal still?" I say. "That's a pity."

She glares at me. It feels good to rattle her. If I'm going to lose the game, I'm not going to be a good loser.

"So, actual guns now," I say. "The cognitive vaccine will be used as a weapon too, by the unscrupulous. To make people hurt other people."

"Joining that peacenik school has turned you into a New Age hippy," she says. "If you knew that you could act without conscience, imagine what you could achieve. No voice in your head holding you back. The world needs people like that."

"I think the world is messed up enough already."

She taps the gun in her lap. "Plenty of terrible things are done to keep us safe in our beds at night. Things which no one really *wants* to do," she says. "The bleeding-heart liberals would rather pretend these things don't go on in the name of protecting us all; but they do. I'm trying to make those things a little easier to bear. For everyone."

"But you're actually hurting people. Your Rent-a-Thug hurt Lena, until she kicked his butt."

"That was unfortunate. Misinformation from Callum. But I'm interested that you care. You care about Lena?"

"Of course I do," I say. "And she has nothing to do

319

with any of this."

"Except that…" Her lip twitches in pleasure. She enjoys putting forward a good hypothesis. "Except that *you* effectively gave her name to Callum rather than your own. *You* put Lena in harm's way. Were you finding her annoying, Jess? Is that why you did such a thing?"

"Of course not. I didn't." *Did I really do that deliberately? Because Lena had scared me that night with the room mix-up, or been selfish once too often?*

"You sent me a book about a scientist creating a monster," she continues. "So what about Hanna? Did you care about her, Jess?"

"You don't know the first thing about Hanna!"

"But I do. I've done my homework in the last few days. Was that your handiwork too?"

Partly. Maybe.

"You may be more of a monster than you think, Jess. We all are, deep down. But now you can move on from any trauma, do anything to get what you want and still live with yourself because I can stop the memories. I can reconsolidate them for you."

Except that she's wrong. It hasn't worked.

"You've pumped drugs into me, lied to me. And for what? If you thought you were creating the perfect memory – one that forgets the bad things we *see* and *do* – then you've failed. Big time. You staged the whole accident. You pushed Mum into the path of the car. Brett was driving. All to prove a theory."

She looks taken aback. "But…"

"What? Your reconsolidation therapy not looking so effective, is it? Your brainwashing a teensy bit reversible?"

Coleman purses her lips and I detect the first traces of doubt.

"You can't stop the feelings – guilt, regret, fear, love," I say. "I can't ever forget what part I may have played in what happened to Hanna. I don't want to."

She prods me with the gun to the back of the car. She points to a large black case. "Open it!"

I do as she asks and look inside: a laptop, memory sticks, papers. I recognize the black notebooks from her study.

"Proof. Proper. Scientific. Proof," she says, spitting out the words.

"Do you think this is proof? Because it isn't. This doesn't prove your theory at all." I tap my chest. "Q.E.D. *Me*, I'm the proof *that it doesn't work*." I grab the laptop and stamp on it before hurling it into the moor, as far as I can throw it, followed by more contents of the case. The notebooks scatter and fall on to the boggy ground. Coleman shrieks and runs after them, leaving the gun resting against the car, her expensive shoes squelching in the peat as she grabs at the cracked laptop and tries to dry it on her skirt. Mud's smeared on her fancy clothes and splattered up her tights. Not so well groomed any more.

"I think you forgot something in all the excitement," I call.

I've got the gun. And I'm pointing it at her.

I take the last manuscript from the case. A set of printed A4 sheets, looking so innocuous. The true *Principles of Memory (Limited Edition)*. It sets out the Programme, those experiments I suffered, her unethical theories, the drugs and the ultimate cognitive vaccine. I can read it myself. See her final version of the truth. I roll it and tuck it inside my jacket, taking care to keep the gun barrels pointed at Coleman at all times.

I advance towards her. Small step by small step. I take one forward, she takes one back, like a slow-motion ballroom dance. She's getting closer and closer to the edge of the bridge. I can see the panic in her eyes. She's trying to judge what kind of monster she created.

I'm trying to judge it too.

She looks around behind her. "The boys will be

back at any minute."

"I don't think they will. *You* sent your driver into the mire. I'm the one with the map in my head, remember! I should think he's rather stuck by now – up to his neck. A bunch of teenagers on a hike are passing fairly near him soon. If he shouts loud enough, someone might hear him."

She glances anxiously to either side.

"Maybe you should go and look for him, as you're so concerned," I say. We're all alone. Me and her. I've dreamed of this moment. Well, not this exact moment. I didn't realize I'd have such a choice of ways to end this. *To kill her*. Shotgun, force her into a bog or make her jump off the bridge into the raging river. All of them are appealing in their own way.

And final.

An eye for an eye.

Which method shall I choose?

I click off the safety catch on the gun. "The problem with being able to remember everything, Professor, is that it can make it awfully hard to forgive."

"Wait!" she shouts. "You don't want to do this."

"Don't I? You're looking rather nervous for someone who knows my brain inside out. You're the cognitive neuroscientist! Can't you tell what I'm going to do?"

"You don't know the full truth about your mother and the accident. You need to listen to me."

"Oh, but I do know the truth," I snarl back.

"Freya, Jess, I…" she splutters.

"Isn't this what you want? People doing terrible things with impunity?" I raise the gun, supporting the butt against the pit of my shoulder, braced for the kick when I fire it, just like I'm back in the college grounds taking out clay pigeons.

Maybe she's right that I can tip her off Ryders Bridge and watch her hit the rocks below and not feel any remorse. After all she's done to me, to Mum, who would blame me? Self-defence. Self-preservation. Justice.

Coleman raises her hands to shield her face. She looks smaller, diminished. Pathetic. A thin, nasty little woman whom I could shatter into a thousand messy pieces. She's still pleading with me, telling me to listen to her.

Memories of Mum and Hanna are thrashing around my head. I half-close my eyes to shut them out and squint down the barrel of the gun, finding the sight. Coleman has stopped moving backwards. She's at the edge of the bridge, casting glances at the turbulent water below. I can see the fear in her face. Good. She deserves this. She brought it on herself. The insistent roar of the river as it crashes over the rocks fills my ears. Her lips are moving but I can't hear her. I move closer.

And suddenly my world turns upside down.

"But she's not dead, Jess," she shouts. "She's not dead!"

Then more quietly, with the assurance of someone who's played a trump card: "Your mother didn't die."

44

Then you will know the truth, and the truth will set you free.

John 8:32

I lower the gun.

"W-what did you say?" I stammer.

"She didn't die, Jess," says Coleman. "She was in an induced coma. But she's still alive."

"You're lying again," I scream. "Stop lying to me." But I'm thinking, thinking. I'm scrolling back through the memories. I'm looking for the thing that doesn't fit, that doesn't feel right.

"It was for the best," she says. "Your mother was causing difficulties, asking awkward questions. You know what she was like." Coleman moves slowly towards me.

"You can't just try to kill someone for being an awkward cow!" I shout. "You really are mad. Stark, raving mad. How's Mum now?"

"She was threatening to go to the press. She was jeopardizing all the good work I'd done – the whole Programme was at stake. I saw an opportunity."

"An *opportunity*?" I'm dizzy and nauseous. *I'm not like Coleman, am I?*

"It went a little further than I'd planned," says Coleman. "All great advances produce collateral damage but one day this experiment of ours will be famous. If I can change your superior memory, I can change anyone's."

Now she's within a metre of me. I can see her lying eyes, the look I'm used to from the lab, taking in my reactions, taking notes, observing me as an animal.

"Where is she?" I shout. "Where's my mum?"

"She's being well looked after. I'm not a monster. She has the best of care."

Coleman *is* a monster. She's turned *herself* into one, not me. Can I believe anything she says? Is this true? "But you told me she was dead. I saw her body," I insist. "We went to the hospital and I saw her body."

"You forced me into that. I'd rather not have gone

through that elaborate charade," she says. "I had to call in favours at the teaching hospital. She still had an IV in her arm under that sheet and the other equipment was under the trolley. We had to be quick and get her back to the unit."

Bodies, Especially After Death, Go Cold, Freya.

The warmth of the body – that's why the window was misted up from the other side. When I saw Mum's body through the glass at the hospital, she was *breathing*. She was still alive. Is that what Desai was hinting at?

"But we scattered her ashes," I say. "I said goodbye."

"Yes: ashes from the hospital incinerator. No one would know the difference. And we had that touching little ceremony on the boat. I was quite teary-eyed."

I think of the inlaid box in my trunk, how I've cherished it and patted it and introduced it to Dan. I was going to take it to New York. Now I know it's the burnt remains of random clinical waste. Body parts, a removed appendix, a set of tonsils? It was never Mum.

"She's showing positive signs of improvement," she says, more softly. "And of course she's always asking after you."

Is she lying? To save her skin. Or is there a chance

it's true? The misted glass. Have I remembered it properly – or is it another distortion? My infallible memory is breaking down. I don't know what the past is any more. Flash-click, erase.

"What do you mean, exactly? How is she?"

"You can see her." She lays her hand gently on my arm. "As soon as we've met my associates."

I don't believe she'll let me. But if there's *any* chance that Mum is alive…

"Hey!" Brett shouts from the direction of the car and runs towards us.

If Brett's OK, that must mean Ramesh Desai isn't. Coleman quickly grabs at the shotgun barrel while I'm distracted by Brett. But I hold on tightly to the stock and we both grapple with it. It fires into the air and the kickback sends it spinning out of our hands. Coleman falls backwards, catching her head on the edge of the wall. The gun lands half on, half off the low parapet of the bridge; rocking slightly before gravity takes over and it tips down into the River Dart below. I can only watch it disappear into the water.

Brett is at Coleman's side, tending to her grazed head. I run to the boot of the car for the potential weapon I saw earlier. Kim's game again. The memory game. The suitcases are still there, the black umbrella, the pack of small bottles of water. The metal wheel wrench for changing tyres was tucked into a tailor-made cavity at the side of the boot. But now it's gone.

I check behind the bags in my panic. Have I misremembered this too?

There's a sound behind me.

"Looking for something?" Brett holds up the tool. He tucks it into his back pocket as he comes closer. He pushes me hard in the chest, sending me sprawling to the ground. I see a figure coming through the mist. A hiker, at last.

"Get away from her!" shouts Dan. My Dan. He's made it to Ryders Bridge. He runs at Brett, swinging his rucksack, sending it full force into him. Brett staggers back briefly before hitting out at Dan. Dan's armed with nothing but a whistle round his neck and a laminated map sticking out of his jacket pocket.

Thwack! Brett's started on Dan, punching him in the face. Dan strikes him back, hitting at his stomach. The next punch from Brett is more brutal. Dan hits the ground.

"Watch out!" I shout as Brett aims a kick at his head, but Dan rolls to one side. He's on all fours shaking himself like a wounded puppy. This time Brett's foot doesn't miss and Dan slumps in a heap. Brett pulls out the wrench from his back pocket. He's going to kill Dan. "No!" I shout, dashing forward.

Brett, feeling the weight of the wrench in his hand, looks over at Coleman, who's still rubbing her head, resting against the bridge.

I'm panicking. The feelings I have for Dan, they're real. He's real. I don't want her staging another accident, with him. "Let him go," I say, "and I'll be your living, walking proof – the ultimate lab rat."

"Young love! How sweet," she snaps, rising to her feet. "I'd like my papers back too. The ones you took."

I still have her final manuscript tucked inside my jacket. Without these papers and the ruined black record books and data, the only evidence I have left is me – I'm the last depository. A flipping Harry Potter Horcrux.

Dan moans and stirs but Brett stamps on his hand. Dan yelps in pain and my stomach flips.

Coleman holds out her hand for the manuscript, a triumphant smile on her lips.

"Here, catch it," I say, charging at her, knocking her back to the ground, smashing her leg against the hard stone. Pages of the manuscript flutter like a flip book, peeling off and scattering. They swoop and fly in the wind, pages catching in the breeze. Some sheets are already in the water, tossing and turning in the Dart, soaking, ink-running, sinking. Her work, my proof, my revenge, washing away. The truth gone.

I fling myself on Brett's back as he's bending towards Dan, who still isn't moving. "Noooooo!" I shout, flailing fists, pulling at his arms. He spins, yanking at my shoulders to pull me off and we tumble to the ground. The wrench skids off into the gorse. Brett's clambering to his feet but I grab his ankle and with all my strength pull him down again. I scramble up to get to Dan. But Brett fills the gap between us.

"You cow," Brett yells. "You're ruining everything."

"No. You did that all by yourself. You're meant to be a scientist with a bit of integrity – not a lapdog, a sad sidekick to Cruella De Vil here."

I try to run but he grabs me.

"This is important research," he says. "This will help us understand the brain more."

"Is that what you're telling yourself to feel better about what you did to me, to Mum? What about your family, Brett – didn't you used to want to research a cure for brain diseases like Alzheimer's or Parkinson's to help people like them? I read your articles. Isn't that what you used to think was important?"

He hesitates.

"This is all about the money for her," I say. "Not the research."

He glances over at Coleman. It's enough; enough for his eyes to flick towards her and his grip to loosen slightly.

"And research shows people like me are lacking in empathy, so feel this!" I take the lesson learned from Lena and deliver three swift moves: a kick to his shin, a drive with both my hands up and through his arms and then a punch driven up into his nose with the flat of my palm, crumpling his septum. One, two, three. I shove him backwards and he falls to the ground, dazed.

I rush to Dan. "Dan! We've got to move." I scrunch up my Hanna's Hike T-shirt and try to stem the bleeding from his hand. "Please, Dan. Please be OK."

His eyes open and he tries to stand, pushing his weight on his arms and falling back. I grab one arm and try to hoist him to his feet. "Get up, Dan, please get up."

Brett stirs and groans.

"Come on, Dan!"

I have to get him away from Brett and Coleman. The map in my mind is as clear as anything. Over Ryders Bridge, path to the left, take the first track to the right with the tor in the background. I can see the contours on the map, the pile of stones. I can work out the distance, even in this fog, I *can* do it.

Dan stands, unsteady. His hand on his head. "Jess, go. Go while you can."

"No. You don't get rid of me that easily." I put my arm round his waist and pull him towards the bridge.

"Didn't I say that to you once?" he says, weakly.

"Yes, and nobody likes a hypocrite, so shut up and move."

I look back. Brett's sitting up, dabbing at his bloody nose. Coleman's limping towards him.

"I'm not leaving you." I jab at the words on Dan's T-shirt – 'Walking together to remember'. His fingers are a pulpy mess. I elevate his hand to limit the bleeding. The first-aid kit's in his rucksack, too close to Brett. I let him lean on me as we shuffle towards the bridge.

"The proof," whispers Dan. "The evidence. You let it go."

"That doesn't matter," I say. "You do. I chose you." *Not revenge. Not a bunch of lies and untruths.* And I know it so clearly, the truth, the honesty of the feelings I have for him, and he has for me.

But he's woozy, his eyes half-closed. Did he even

hear what I said? I need him to stay awake, to keep going. To survive.

Brett's back on his feet. He's moving towards the wrench.

We're halfway across the bridge. "Come on, Dan. I want to introduce you to my mum, for real this time."

"What? I don't…" He stumbles and I struggle to hold him up.

"Aaaaaarrrgh!" Brett's coming at us, full throttle, holding the metal tool above his head. I try to shield Dan with my body but Brett ploughs into both of us like a battering ram. I grab at Brett's shirt to regain my footing but he's off balance too and falls with us. We tumble, catching on the tiny parapet which gives way in a crash of stones and mortar. We all fall backwards from the bridge. The three of us in a tangle of flailing limbs, tumbling down into the river.

I try to judge the distance and hold my breath but it's over in an instant, a split second. The coldness of the river shocks me as I strike it. Bubbles everywhere in the murky water. I try to kick up towards the surface. I push the panic down and pretend I'm in the calm blue swimming pool at Dartmeet. I've dived in and I need to get back up, up to the light. I hold my breath like I'm swimming a length at midnight. But the current's dragging me, pulling at me. My hair's over my face and I can't tell which way is up. I strike a rock and graze my cheek. I need to help Dan. He's too injured to swim. And I need to get out of here to help Mum. I can see a dark shape above me breaking the surface. Is it Dan? Is he OK?

My chest's tightening. I need to breathe air. I know the river. I remember the canoe trip with Hanna. We're near the rapids, the run of rushing water over dangerous rocks. I need to swim. I need to live.

This is a time of life and death when people say their life flashes before them. A video of a whole life lived is being played, fast-forward.

I've been living like that for a long time, watching movies of the past. Reliving the past.

But now I want the future.

I'm playing one last movie in my head. It's in slow motion, as though I have all the time in the world to remember. Mum's laughing as she lights the candles on my birthday cake. I can smell the perfume, see the red of her lipstick. She's smiling. "Make a wish, my sweet, make a wish."

45

Play the game: Take a tray of items. A red lipstick, a Danish jumper, a make-up bag, a misted window, a black notebook, a wrench, a one-eyed teddy, a pair of earrings (broken), a candle. Cover them with a shroud. Can you remember them?

Work Your Memory

Someone's grabbing at my arms, pulling. The cold of the water's numbing my senses. I'm slow, half-dead.

"We've got you, love," says a man in a high-vis lifejacket and a helmet. "You're going to be all right, stay with me." They're wrapping me in a foil blanket, rubbing my limbs. It hurts. Everything hurts.

"Dan?" I whisper. "Dan?"

And then I can feel myself go, slipping away.

46

We know so little still about the science of forgetting. And yet the key to good mental health is finding the perfect balance between forgetting and remembering. Whether that's achievable is another matter.

Principles of Memory (Limited Edition) – *Professor A.E. Coleman*

I wake.

Is it night or day?

The room has no windows. The bright strip lighting above me hurts my eyes. I blink.

I move my arm but I'm attached to a drip and a machine that beeps. My other arm feels heavy, constricted. My throat hurts.

A police officer sits in a chair at the side of the bed, fiddling idly with a box of tissues. I try to speak but no sound comes out, only a croak. She leaps up and presses a button on the wall.

A nurse bustles in. "Hello there. Welcome back to the land of the living." She's all efficiency and clipboards and uniform. She shines a light into my eyes and takes notes from the machines. "Doctor's on her way," she says, giving me a sip of water and gently wiping my mouth. "Someone on the surgical ward's been asking after you. He's gone up to theatre."

The police officer gets out her notebook. She shakes her pen and scribbles with it to get the ink flowing. I shut my eyes again and listen to the scratching on the paper.

"You've had a nasty accident," she says. "Seems you fell from Ryders Bridge and got swept downstream."

"You got knocked about and had a few blows to the head from the rocks," adds the nurse. "And your left wrist is fractured." She squeezes my other hand. "But you're safe now," she says. "Cuts and bruises soon heal. You're one of the lucky ones."

My head's buzzing. I want it to stop. I open my eyes and squint up at their faces.

"So question one: what's your name?" asks the police officer. They both stand there expectantly. She repeats herself more slowly like I'm a small child: "Do you know who you are? What's your name?"

"It's…" I stop.

The inside of my head's completely blank.

I can't remember.

I clench the sheet in my fist as the panic rises.

A tall young man with gingery hair that flops over his eyes comes into the room. He has cuts and bruises on his face but still manages to look cute. His bandaged hand touches his ribs. I see the twinge of pain in his face as he sits on the bed. He smiles at me, like he knows me, and the freckles on his nose crinkle.

"Hey, memory girl," he says, and gently strokes my arm.

Scattered memories return, blurred at first, and then swimming into focus. Each one laid next to the other like the most brilliant mosaic. The touch of a hand on my cheek at the pool sending tingles through my body. Dancing round musty clothing rails; running in and out of waves; laughing. Dashing through cloisters in a wedding dress; resting my head on a warm chest in the dark; clasped hands. He's on the moor, standing up for me. I'm standing up for him. Dan and Jess. Jess and Dan.

The pattern of memories grows: red lipstick on smiling lips; a tiled floor and a hat stand; a white car; a misted window; a body under a sheet. A beautiful girl with white-blond hair. All sliding back into position, back to where they should be, where I *want* them to be.

Desai was right. The good and the bad memories shape me. I don't want to shed my history, because I'm sure the good can outweigh the bad. I'll do something important with all I know, with the way I am. Something unforgettable. Starting here.

"You're going to need a bigger notebook," I tell the police officer. "I've got a lot to say."

Acknowledgements

I've always been fascinated by memory. The idea of a girl who could remember everything and the effect that would have on her psyche first popped into my head in a workshop on my MA. She wouldn't let me forget her and evolved into the main character in *The Truth About Lies*.

I should stress this a work of fiction and I've taken my limited knowledge on memory and recent developments gleaned largely from *New Scientist* magazine and twisted it all to fit the story. In the course of writing the book, I got hooked on some of the memory techniques I describe – not enough to enter the UK Memory Championship but enough to remember my PIN numbers at last.

No book is a solo effort. Massive thank you to Ruth Bennett at Stripes for taking a punt on a debut author and helping me through the process along with Rachel Boden, editing supremo. And to the very helpful copy-editor, Anna Bowles, and to Sophie Bransby for her stunning cover design. And to the whole Stripes gang of Lauren, Charlie, Beth and Stephanie who welcomed me with open arms and gingerbread for the *I'll Be Home for Christmas* anthology. And to my lovely agent Jo Williamson who always seems to know when I need a 'Don't Panic' email.

The MA Writing for Young People at Bath Spa got me writing after all these years of only dreaming about it. Big thanks to those who tutored me – Julia Green, Steve Voake, Janine Amos, John McLay, Elen Caldecott and David Almond. Thanks to Marcus Sedgwick who gave me a confidence boost when I needed it. The MA leads you into a mutually supportive alumni and I am forever bound with my super-talented MA workshop gang – Mel, Wendy, Sarah, Jennifer, Jas, Miranda, Charlotte and Sam M. You know who your writing buddies really are when you make them read your first draft so massive thanks to Ele, Laura, Emma, Wendy and Christine. And thanks for all the support from the South-West SCBWIs and the Teaspooners.

Big thank you to all those people who've let me cross-examine them on subjects ranging from pharmacology to shotguns. And to Dr Josh P. Davis for reading the draft to reassure me that I knew my amygdala from my hippocampus.

On a personal note, thanks to the caring folk at the Royal United Hospital in Bath who were busy patching me up when I'd hoped to be putting the finishing touches to the book. And to the army of brilliant friends who wheeled me around and kept me supplied with chocolate.

Lastly to my family. So sad that neither my parents nor my big brother are around to share the moment, but to Tricia and Pete, my lifetime support network; thank you.

Thanks to my boys, James and Ally, who inspire and encourage in equal measure. Ally with his amazing memory is my research guru. And lastly to my husband Dolf who has supported me unconditionally and always knows where to stick an apostrophe.

Never forget a face?

Like Callum and Jess, I have an aptitude for recognizing faces and I've been part of a super-recognizer research programme. Luckily Dr Josh P. Davis at the University of Greenwich is nothing like Professor Coleman and the research has been a pleasure for a memory geek like me.

So I've been looking at photos of faces, and then picking out that person from a group of facial images. Sounds easy, but it gets progressively harder when they're wearing a hat or glasses or seen from a different angle or the photo is blurry and pixelated, like a terrible CCTV image. I'm instinctively checking out the jawline, dimples, hairline, the position of the eyes, the shape of the earlobes. I seem to find the tests with faces easier than the ones with objects. I'm also part of a family study with my children looking at whether good facial recognition runs in families and if there's a correlation with shyness. Are introverts better at recognizing than extroverts?

The Met Police in London really does have a super-recognizer unit who have a natural talent, way beyond my capabilities, for recognizing faces. They're particularly useful for crowd events like sports matches and concerts where the mass of people makes it more difficult for CCTV and software to pick up known troublemakers. Whether humans will outstrip technology for much longer remains to be seen.

So how good are *you* at remembering faces? Do you easily spot minor actors in their latest TV show? Do you recognize on the street people you've only briefly met before?

You can test yourself here to see if you too have what it takes:

https://tinyurl.com/yc575sdh

About the Author

Tracy Darnton graduated with Distinction from the Bath Spa MA Writing for Young People. She originally studied law at Cambridge and has worked as a solicitor and law lecturer. Tracy won the Stripes YA Short Story Prize in 2016, run in partnership with *The Bookseller*'s YA Book Prize, which led to inclusion in the *I'll Be Home for Christmas* YA anthology.

Tracy lives in Bath with her husband and two sons.

@TracyDarnton